The Long March

AND

In the Clap Shack

ALSO BY *William Styron*

Lie Down in Darkness
Set This House on Fire
The Confessions of Nat Turner
Sophie's Choice
This Quiet Dust
Darkness Visible

The
Long
March

AND

In the
Clap Shack

William Styron

VINTAGE INTERNATIONAL
VINTAGE BOOKS
A DIVISION OF RANDOM HOUSE, INC.
NEW YORK

c. 3

FIRST VINTAGE INTERNATIONAL EDITION, JANUARY 1993

The Long March *copyright © 1952 by William Styron*
In the Clap Shack *copyright © 1973 by William Styron*

All rights reserved under International and Pan-American Copyright
Conventions. Published in the United States by Vintage Books, a
division of Random House, Inc., New York, and simultaneously in
Canada by Random House of Canada Limited, Toronto.
The Long March was originally published in 1952 in *Discovery*
magazine and in 1956 by The Modern Library.
In the Clap Shack was originally published in hardcover by Random
House, Inc., New York, in 1973.

CAUTION: Professionals and amateurs are hereby warned that *In the
Clap Shack*, being fully protected under the Copyright Laws of the
United States of America, the British Commonwealth, including the
Dominion of Canada, and all other countries of the Berne and Universal
Copyright Conventions, is subject to royalty. All rights, including professional, amateur, recording, motion picture, recitation, lecturing,
public reading, radio and television broadcasting, and the rights of
translation into foreign languages, are strictly reserved, permission for
which must be secured in writing from the author's agent: Harold Mat-
son Company, Inc., 22 East 40th St., New York, New York, 10016.
Particular emphasis is laid on the question of readings.

Library of Congress Cataloging-in-Publication Data
Styron, William, 1925–
    [Long march]
    The long march; and, In the clap shack / William Styron. — 1st
Vintage International ed.
      p.   cm.
    The long march originally published: New York: The Modern
    Library, 1956, © 1952; In the clap shack originally published:
    New York: Random House, 1973.
    ISBN 0-679-73675-1 (pbk.)
    I. Styron, William, 1925– In the clap shack. 1992. II. Title.
III. Title: Long march. IV. Title: In the clap shack.
PS3569.T9L6   1993
813'.54—dc20   92-56371
                CIP

Manufactured in the United States of America
10 9 8 7 6 5 4 3 2 1

The Long March

to

Hiram Haydn

ONE NOON, in the blaze of a cloud-less Carolina summer, what was left of eight dead boys lay strewn about the landscape, among the poison ivy and the pine needles and loblolly saplings. It was not so much as if they had departed this life but as if, sprayed from a hose, they were only shreds of bone, gut, and dangling tissue to which it would have been impossible ever to impute the quality of life, far less the capacity to relinquish it. Of course, though, these had really died quickly, no doubt before the faintest flicker of recognition, of wonder, apprehension, or terror had had time to register in their minds. But the shock, it occurred to Lieutenant Culver, who stood in the shady lee of an ambulance and watched the scene, must have been fantastic to those on the periphery of the explosion, those fifteen or so surviving marines who now lay on the ground beneath blankets, moaning with pain and fright, and who, not more than half an hour before, had been waiting patiently in line for their lunch before the two mortar shells, misfired—how? why? the question already hung with a buzzing, palpable fury in the noontime heat—had plummeted down upon the chow-line and had deadened their ears and senses and had hurled them earthward where they lay now, alive but stricken in a welter of blood and brain, scattered messkits and mashed potatoes, and puddles of melting ice cream. Moments ago in the confusion—just before he had stolen off from the Colonel's side to go behind a tree and get sick—Lieutenant Culver had had a glimpse of a young sweaty face grimed with dust, had heard the boy's voice, astonishing even in that moment of nausea because of its clear, unhysterical tone of explanation: "Major, I tell you I was on the field phone and I tell you as soon as they come out the tube I knew they were short rounds and so I hollered . . ." Of course it had been an accident. But why? He heard the Major shout something, then Culver had heard no more, retching on the leaves with a sound that, for the moment, drowned out the cries and whines of the wounded and the noise of trucks and ambulances crashing up through the underbrush.

It was not that he had a weak stomach or that he was unacquainted with carnage that allowed him to lose control. If anything, he prided himself on his stomach, and as for blood he had seen a lot spilled on Okinawa and had himself (although through no act of valor whatever) received a shrapnel wound —in the buttocks, a matter which even in retrospect, as he had often been forced to remind his wife, possessed no elements of comedy at all. In this case it was simply that on the one hand he himself had been shocked. The sight of death was the sort of thing which in wartime is expected, which one protects one-

self against, and which is finally excused or
ıt least ignored, in the same way that a beg-
gar is ignored, or a head cold, or a social
problem. But in training here in the States in
peacetime (or what, this sweltering summer
in the early 1950s, passed as peacetime) one
had felt no particular need for that type of
self-defense, and the slick nude litter of in-
testine and shattered blue bones, among which
forks and spoons peeked out like so many
pathetic metal flowers, made a crazy, insult-
ing impact at Culver's belly, like the blow of
a fist. And on the other hand (and the pulsing
ache at his brow now as he vomited helplessly
onto his shoes lent confirmation to what he'd
been trying to deny to himself for months):
he was too old, he was no longer an eager kid
just out of Quantico with a knife between
his teeth. He was almost thirty, he was old,
and he was afraid.

Lieutenant Culver had been called back to
the marines early that spring. When, one Saturday morning, his wife had thrown the
brown envelope containing his orders onto the
bed where he lay sleeping, he experienced an
odd distress which kept him wandering about,

baffled and mumbling to himself, for days. Like most of his fellow reserves he had retained his commission after the last war. It was an insouciant gesture which he had assumed would in some way benefit him in case of an all-out conflict, say, thirty years hence, but one which made no provisions for such an eventuality as a police action in Korea. It had all come much too soon and Culver had felt weirdly as if he had fallen asleep in some barracks in 1945 and had awakened in a half-dozen years or so to find that the intervening freedom, growth, and serenity had been only a glorious if somewhat prolonged dream. A flood of protest had welled up in him, for he had put the idea of war out of his mind entirely, and the brief years since Okinawa had been the richest of his life. They had produced, among lesser things, a loving, tenderly passionate wife who had passed on to their little girl both some of her gentle nature and her wealth of butter-colored hair; a law degree, the fruits of which he had just begun to realize, even though still somewhat impecuniously, as one of the brightest juniors in a good New York law firm; a friendly beagle named Howard whom he took for hikes in Washington Square; a cat, whom he did not deign to call by name, and despised; and a record-player that played Haydn, Mozart and Bach.

Up until the day that his orders came— the day that he tried to forget and the one that Betsy, his wife, soon bitterly referred to as "the day the roof fell in"—they had been living in a roomy walk-up in the Village and experiencing the prosaic contentment that comes from eating properly, indulging themselves with fair moderation in the pleasures of the city, and watching the growth of a child. This is not to say that they were either smug or dull. They had a bright circle of friends, mostly young lawyers and newspapermen and doctors and their wives. There were parties and occasional week ends in the country, where everyone became frankly drunk. There were the usual household skirmishes, too, but these were infrequent and petered out quickly. Both of them were too sensible to allow some domestic misdemeanor to develop into anything horrible; they were well adjusted and each of them found it easy to admit, long after the honeymoon, that they were deeply in love. Months later at camp, ensnared futilely in the coils of some administrative flypaper, Culver would find himself gazing up from his work and out across the smoky hot barrens of pine and sand, relieving his vast boredom in a daydream of that vanished simplicity and charm. His mind seemed to drift toward one recurrent vision. This was of the afternoons in winter when—bundled to the ears, the baby-carriage joggling bravely in the van and the melancholy beagle scampering at their heels—they took their Sunday stroll. On such days the city, its frantic heartbeat quieted and clothed in the sooty white tatters of a recent snow, seemed to have an Old World calm, and the people that passed them in the twilight appeared to be, like themselves, pink-cheeked and contented, no matter what crimson alarms flowered at the newsstands or what evil rumors sounded from distant radios. For Culver the waning Sunday light had not spelled out the promise of Monday morning's gloom but of Monday's challenge—and this was not because he was a go-getter but because he was happy. He was happy to walk through the chill and leafless dusk with his wife and his child and his dog. And he was happy to return home to warmth and peanut butter and liverwurst, to the familiar delight of the baby's good-night embrace, to the droll combat between beagle and cat, to music before sleep. Sometimes in these reveries Culver thought that it was the music, more than anything, which provided the key, and he recalled himself at a time which already seemed dark ages ago, surrounded by beer cans and attuned, in the nostalgic air of a winter evening, to some passage from some forgotten Haydn. It was one happy and ascending bar that he remembered, a dozen bright notes through which he passed in memory to an earlier, untroubled day at the end of childhood. There, like tumbling flowers against the sunny grass, their motions as nimble as the music itself, two lovely little girls played tennis, called to him voicelessly, as in a dream, and waved their arms.

The sordid little town outside the camp possessed the horror of recognition, for Culver had been there before. They left the baby with a sister and headed South where, on the outskirts of the town, they found a cramped room in a tourist cabin. They were there for two weeks. They searched vainly for a place to live, there was no more room at the camp. They turned away from bleak cell-like rooms offered at five times their value, were shown huts and chicken-coops by characters whose bland country faces could not hide the sparkle, in their calculating eyes, of venal lust. The aging proprietress of the tourist camp was a scold and a cheat. And so they finally gave up. Betsy went home. He kissed her good-by late one rainy afternoon in the bus station, surrounded by a horde of marines and by cheap suitcases and fallen candy wrappers and the sound of fretful children—all of the unlovely mementoes, so nightmarishly familiar, of leave-taking and of anxiety. Of war. He felt her tears against his cheek. It had been an evil day, and the rain that streamed against the windows, blurring a distant frieze of gaunt gray pines, had seemed to nag with both remembrance and foreboding—of tropic seas, storm-swept distances and strange coasts.

II

He had heard the explosion himself. They had been eating at their own chow-line in a command post set up in a grove of trees, when the noise came from off to the right, distant enough but still too close: a twin quick earth-shaking sound—*crump crump*. Then seconds later in the still of noon when even the birds had become quiet and only a few murmured voices disturbed the concentration of eating, a shudder had passed through the surrounding underbrush, like a faint hot wind. It was premonitory, perhaps, but still no one knew. The leaves rustled, ceased, and Culver had looked up from where he squatted against a tree to see fifty scattered faces peering toward the noise, their knives and forks suspended. Then from the galley among the trees a clatter broke the silence, a falling pan or kettle, and someone laughed, and the Colonel, sitting nearby, had said to the Major—what had he said? Culver couldn't remember, yet there had been something uneasy in his tone, even then, before anyone had known, and at least ten minutes before the radio corporal, a tobacco-chewing clown from Oklahoma named Hobbs, came trotting up brushing crumbs from his mouth, a message book clutched in one fat paw. He was popular in battalion headquarters, one of those favored men who, through some simplicity or artlessness of nature, can manage a profane familiarity which in another would be insubordinate; the look of concern on his clown's face, usually so whimsical, communicated an added dread.

"I gotta flash red from Plumbob, Colonel, and it ain't no problem emergency. All hell's broke loose over in Third Battalion. They dropped in some short rounds on a chow-line and they want corpsmen and a doctor and the chaplain. Jesus, you should hear 'em down there."

The Colonel had said nothing at first. The brief flicker of uneasiness in his eyes had fled, and when he put down his messkit and looked up at Hobbs it was only to wipe his hands on his handkerchief and squint casually into the sun, as if he were receiving the most routine of messages. It was absolutely

typical of the man, Culver reflected. Too
habitual to be an act yet still somehow too
faintly self-conscious to be entirely natural,
how many years and what strange interior
struggle had gone into the perfection of such
a gesture? It was good, Grade-A Templeton,
perhaps not a distinctly top-notch perform-
ance but certainly, from where the critic Culver sat, deserving of applause: the frail, lit-
tle-boned, almost pretty face peering upward
with a look of attitudinized contemplation;
the pensive bulge of tongue sliding inside the
rim of one tanned cheek to gouge out some
particle of food; small hands working calmly
in the folds of the handkerchief—surely all
this was more final, more commanding than
the arrogant loud mastery of a Booth, more
like the skill of Bernhardt, who could cow
men by the mystery of her smallest twitch.
Perhaps fifteen seconds passed before he
spoke. Culver became irritated—at his own
suspense, throbbing inside him like a heartbeat, and at the awesome silence which, as if
upon order, had fallen over the group of five,
detached from the bustle of the rest of the
command post: the Colonel; Hobbs; Major

Lawrence, the executive officer, now gazing
at the Colonel with moist underlip and defer-
ential anxiety; Captain Mannix; himself.
Back off in the bushes a mockingbird com-
menced a shrill rippling chant and far away,
amidst the depth of the silence, there seemed
to be a single faint and terrible scream.
Hobbs spat an auburn gob of tobacco-juice
into the sand, and the Colonel spoke: "Let me
have that radio, Hobbs, and get me Plumbob
One," he said evenly, and then with no change
of tone to the Major: "Billy, send a runner
over for Doc Patterson and you two get down
there with the chaplain. Take my jeep. Tell
the Doc to detach all his corpsmen. And you'd
better chop-chop."

The Major scrambled to his feet. He was
youthful and handsome, a fine marine in his
polished boots, his immaculate dungarees—
donned freshly clean, Culver had observed,
that morning. He was of the handsomeness
preferred by other military men—regular
features, clean-cut, rather athletic—but there
was a trace of peacetime fleshiness in his
cheeks which often lent to the corners of his
mouth a sort of petulance, so that every now

and again, his young uncomplicated face in deep concentration over some operations map or training schedule or order, he looked like a spoiled and arrogant baby of five. "Aye-aye, sir," he said and bent over the Colonel, bestowing upon him that third-person flattery which to Culver seemed perilously close to bootlicking and was thought to be considerably out of date, especially among the reserves. "Does the Colonel want us to run our own problem as ordered, sir?" He was a regular.

Templeton took the headset from Hobbs, who lowered the radio down beside him in the sand. "Yeah, Billy," he said, without looking up, "yeah, that'll be all right. We'll run her on time. Tell O'Leary to tell all companies to push off at thirteen-hundred."

"Aye-aye, sir." And the Major, boots sparkling, was off in a puff of pine needles and dust.

"Jesus," Mannix said. He put down his messkit and nudged Culver in the ribs. Captain Mannix, the commanding officer of headquarters company, was Culver's friend and, for five months, his closest one. He was a dark heavy-set Jew from Brooklyn, Culver's age and a reserve, too, who had had to sell his radio store and leave his wife and two children at home. He had a disgruntled sense of humor which often seemed to bring a spark of relief not just to his own, but to Culver's, feeling of futility and isolation. Mannix was a bitter man and, in his bitterness, sometimes recklessly vocal. He had long ago given up genteel accents, and spoke like a marine. It was easier, he maintained. "Je-*sus*," he whispered again, too loud, "what'll Congress do about this? Look at Billy chop-chop."

Culver said nothing. His tension eased off a bit, and he looked around him. The news had not seemed yet to have spread around the command post; the men began to get up and walk to the chow-line to clean their mess-gear, strolled back beneath the trees and flopped down, heads against their packs, for a moment's nap. The Colonel spoke in an easy, confidential voice with the other battalion commander: the casualties were confined, Culver gathered, to that outfit. It was a battalion made up mostly of young reserves and it was one in which, he suddenly thanked

God, he knew no one. Then he heard the
Colonel go on calmly—to promise more aid,
to promise to come down himself, shortly.
"Does it look rough, Luke?" Culver heard
him say, "Hold on tight, Luke boy"—all in
the cool and leisurely, almost bored, tones of
a man to whom the greatest embarrassment
would be a show of emotion, and to whom,
because of this quality, had been given, in
the midst of some strained and violent combat
situation long ago, the name "Old Rocky."
He was not yet forty-five, yet the adjective
"old" applied, for there was a gray sheen in
his hair and a bemused, unshakable look in
his tranquil eyes that made him seem, like
certain young ecclesiastics, prematurely aged
and perhaps even wise. Culver saw him put
the headset down and get up, walking off toward the operations tent with a springy, slim-
hipped, boyish stride, calling out over his
shoulder as he went: "Mannix." Simply that:
Mannix. A voice neither harsh nor peremp-
tory nor, on the other hand, particularly
gentle. It was merely a voice which expected
to be obeyed, and Culver felt Mannix's big
weight against him as the Captain put a hand

on his shoulder and pried himself up from the ground, muttering, "Jesus, lemme digest a bit, Jack."

Mannix despised the Colonel. Yet, Culver thought, as the Captain hulked stiff-kneed behind the Colonel and disappeared after him into the operations tent, Mannix despised everything about the Marine Corps. In this attitude he was like nearly all the reserves, it was true, but Mannix was more noisily frank in regard to his position. He detested Templeton not because of any slight or injustice, but because Templeton was a lieutenant colonel, because he was a regular, and because he possessed over Mannix—after six years of freedom—an absolute and unquestioned authority. Mannix would have hated any battalion commander, had he the benignity of Santa Claus, and Culver, listening to Mannix's frequently comical but often too audible complaints, as just now, was kept in a constant state of mild suspense—half amusement, half horror. Culver settled himself against the tree. Apparently there was nothing, for the moment at least, that he could do. Above him an airplane droned through the stillness. A truck grumbled across the clearing, carrying a group of languid hospital corpsmen, was gone; around him the men lay against their packs in crumpled attitudes of sleep. A heavy drowsiness came over him, and he let his eyes slide closed. Suddenly he yearned, with all of the hunger of a schoolboy in a classroom on a May afternoon, to be able to collapse into slumber. For the three days they had been on the problem he had averaged only four hours of sleep a night— almost none last night—and gratefully he knew he'd be able to sleep this evening. He began to doze, dreaming fitfully of home, of white cottages, of a summer by the sea. *Long walk tonight.* And his eyes snapped open then —on what seemed to be the repeated echo, from afar, of that faint anguished shriek he had heard before—in the horrid remembrance that there would be no sleep tonight. For anyone at all. Only a few seconds had passed.

"Long walk tonight," the voice repeated. Culver stared upward through a dazzling patchwork of leaves and light to see the broad pink face of Sergeant O'Leary, smiling down.

"Christ, O'Leary," he said, "don't remind me."

The Sergeant, still grinning, gestured with his shoulder in the direction of the operations tent. "The Colonel's really got a wild hair, ain't he?" He chuckled and reached down and clutched one of his feet, with an elaborate groan.

Culver abruptly felt cloaked in a gloom that was almost tangible, and he was in no mood to laugh. "You'll be really holding that foot tomorrow morning," he said, "and that's no joke."

The grin persisted. "Ah, Mister Culver," O'Leary said, "don't take it so hard. It's just a little walk through the night. It'll be over before you know it." He paused, prodding with his toe at the pine needles. "Say," he went on, "what's this I heard about some short rounds down in Third Batt?"

"I don't know from nothing, O'Leary. I just read the papers." Another truck came by, loaded with corpsmen, followed by a jeep in

which sat the helmeted Major Lawrence, a
look of sulky arrogance on his face, his arms
folded at his chest like a legionnaire riding
through a conquered city. "But from what I
understand," Culver went on, turning back,
"quite a few guys got hurt."

"That's tough," O'Leary said. "I'll bet
you they were using that old stuff they've had
stored on Guam ever since '45. Jesus, you'd
think they'd have better sense. Why, I seen
those shells stacked up high as a man out
there just last year, getting rained on every
day and getting the jungle rot and Jesus, they
put tarps over 'em but five years is one hell
of a long time to let 81-shells lay around. I
remember once . . ." Culver let him talk,
without hearing the words, and drowsed.
O'Leary was an old-timer (though only a few
years older than Culver), a regular who had
just signed over for four more years, and it
was impossible to dislike him. On Guadal-
canal he had been only a youngster, but in
the intervening years the Marine Corps had
molded him—perhaps by his own unconscious choice—in its image, and he had become as inextricably grafted to the system as

any piece of flesh surgically laid on to arm or thigh. There was great heartiness and warmth in him but at the same time he performed all infantry jobs with a devoted, methodical competence. He could say sarcastically, "The Colonel's really got a wild hair, ain't he?" but shrug his shoulders and grin, and by that ambivalent gesture sum up an attitude which only a professional soldier could logically retain: I doubt the Colonel's judgment a little, but I will willingly do what he says. He also shared with Hobbs, the radioman, some sort of immunity. And thus it had been last night, Culver recalled, that upon the Colonel's announcement about this evening's forced march—which was to take thirteen hours and extend the nearly thirty-six miles back to the main base—O'Leary had been able to give a long, audible, incredulous whistle, right in the Colonel's face, and elicit from the Colonel an indulgent smile; whereas in the same blackout tent and at virtually the same instant Mannix had murmured, "Thirty-six miles, Jesus Christ," in a tone, however, laden with no more disbelief or no more pain than O'Leary's whistle, and

Culver had seen the Colonel's smile vanish, replaced on the fragile little face by a subtle, delicate shadow of irritation.

"You think that's too long?" the Colonel had said to Mannix then, turning slightly. There had been no hostility in his voice, or even reproof; it had, in fact, seemed merely a question candidly stated—although this might have been because two enlisted men had been in the tent, O'Leary, and some wizened, anonymous little private shivering over the radio. It was midsummer, but nights out in the swamps were fiercely, illogically cold, and from where they had set up the operations tent that evening—on a tiny patch of squashy marshland—the dampness seemed to ooze up and around them, clutching their bones in a chill which extra sweaters and field jackets and sweatshirts could not dislodge. A single kerosene pressure-lamp dangled from overhead—roaring like a pint-sized, encapsuled hurricane; it furnished the only light in the tent, and the negligible solace of a candlelike heat. It had the stark, desperate, manufactured quality of the light one imagines in an execution chamber; under it the Colonel's face, in absolute repose as he stared down for a brief, silent instant and awaited Mannix's reply, looked like that of a mannequin, chalky, exquisite, solitary beneath a store-window glare.

"No, sir," Mannix said. He had recovered quickly. He peered up at the Colonel from his camp stool, expressionless. "No, sir," he repeated, "I don't think it's too long, but it's certainly going to be some hike."

The Colonel did something with his lips. It seemed to be a smile. He said nothing—bemused and mystifying—wearing the enigma of the moment like a cape. In the silence the tempestuous little lamp boiled and raged; far off in the swamp somewhere a mortar flare flew up with a short, sharp crack. O'Leary broke the quietness in the tent with a loud sneeze, followed, almost like a prolongation of the sneeze, by a chuckle, and said: "Oh boy, Colonel, there're gonna be some sore feet Saturday morning."

The Colonel didn't answer. He hooked his thumbs in his belt. He turned to the Major, who was brooding upward from the field desk, cheeks propped against his hands. "I was sitting in my tent a while ago, Billy," the Colonel said, "and I got to thinking. I got to thinking about a lot of things. I got to thinking about the Battalion. I said to myself, 'How's the Battalion doing?' I mean, 'What kind of an outfit do I have here? Is it in good combat shape? If we were to meet an Aggressor enemy tomorrow would we come out all right?' Those were the queries I posed to myself. Then I tried to formulate an answer." He paused, his eyes luminous and his lips twisted in a wry, contemplative smile as if he were indeed, again, struggling with the weight of the questions to which he had addressed himself. The Major was absorbed; he looked up at Templeton with an intent baby-blue gaze and parted mouth, upon which, against a pink cleft of the lower lip, there glittered a bead of saliva. "Reluctantly," the Colonel went on slowly, "reluctantly, I came to this conclusion: the Battalion's been doping off." He paused again. "Doping off. Especially," he said, turning briefly toward Mannix with a thin smile, "a certain component unit known as Headquarters and Service Company." He leaned back on the camp stool

and slowly caressed the pewter-colored surface of his hair. "I decided a little walk
might be in order for tomorrow night, after
we secure the problem. Instead of going back
to the base on the trucks. What do you think,
Billy?"

"I think that's an excellent idea, sir. An
excellent idea. In fact I've been meaning to
suggest something like that to the Colonel for
quite some time. As a means of inculcating a
sort of group *esprit*."

"It's what they need, Billy."

"Full marching order, sir?" O'Leary put
in seriously.

"No, that'd be a little rough."

"Aaa-h," O'Leary said, relieved.

Suddenly Culver heard Mannix's voice:
"Even so—"

"Even so, what?" the Colonel interrupted.
Again, the voice was not hostile, only antici-
patory, as if it already held the answer to
whatever Mannix might ask or suggest.

"Well, even so, Colonel," Mannix went on
mildly, while Culver, suddenly taut and concerned, held his breath, "even without packs
thirty-six miles is a long way for anybody,

much less for guys who've gone soft for the past five or six years. I'll admit my company isn't the hottest outfit in the world, but most of them are reserves—"

"Wait a minute, Captain, wait a minute," the Colonel said. Once more the voice—as cool and as level as the marshy ground upon which they were sitting—carefully skirted any tone of reproach and was merely explicit: "I don't want you to think I'm taking it out on the Battalion merely because of you, or rather H & S Company. But they aren't reserves. They're *marines. Comprend?*" He arose from the chair. "I think," he went on flatly, almost gently, "that there's one thing that we are all tending to overlook these days. We've been trying to differentiate too closely between two particular bodies of men that make up the Marine Corps. Technically it's true that a lot of these new men are reserves—that is, they have an 'R' affixed at the end of the 'USMC.' But it's only a technical difference, you see. Because first and foremost they're *marines.* I don't want my marines doping off. They're going to *act* like marines. They're going to be *fit.* If they

meet an Aggressor enemy next week they
might have to march a long, long way. And
that's what I want this hike to teach them.
Comprend?" He made what could pass for
the token of a smile and laid his hand easily
and for a lingering second on Mannix's shoulder, in a sort of half-gesture of conciliation,
understanding—something—it was hard to
tell. It was an odd picture because from
where he sat Culver was the only one in the
tent who could see, at the same instant, both
of their expressions. In the morbid, comfortless light they were like classical Greek
masks, made of chrome or tin, reflecting an
almost theatrical disharmony: the Colonel's
fleeting grin sculpted cleanly and prettily in
the unshadowed air above the Captain's dark-
ened, downcast face where, for a flicker of
a second, something outraged and agonized
was swiftly graven and swiftly scratched out.
The Colonel's smile was not complacent or
unfriendly. It was not so much as if he had
achieved a triumph but merely equilibrium,
had returned once more to that devout, ordered state of communion which the Captain's words had ever so briefly disturbed. At

that moment Culver almost liked the Colonel,
in some negative way which had nothing to
do with affection, but to which "respect,"
though he hated the word, was the nearest approach. At least it was an honest smile, no
matter how faint. It was the expression of a
man who might be fatuous and a ham of
sorts, but was not himself evil or unjust—a
man who would like to overhear some sergeant say, "He keeps a tight outfit, but he's
straight." In men like Templeton all emo-
tions—all   smiles,   all   anger—emanated
from a priestlike, religious fervor, throbbing inwardly with the cadence of parades
and booted footfalls. By that passion rebels
are ordered into quick damnation but simple doubters sometimes find indulgence—
depending upon the priest, who may be one
inclined toward mercy, or who is one ever
rapt in some litany of punishment and court-
martial. The Colonel was devout but inclined
toward mercy. He was not a tyrant, and his
smile was a sign that the Captain's doubts
were forgiven, probably even forgotten. But
only Culver had seen the Captain's face: a
quick look of both fury and suffering, like the

tragic Greek mask, or a shackled slave. Then
Mannix flushed. "Yes, sir," he said.

The Colonel walked toward the door. He
seemed already to have put the incident out
of his mind. "Culver," he said, "if you can
ever make radio contact with Able Company
tell them to push off at 0600. If you can't,
send a runner down before dawn to see if
they've got the word." He gave the side of
his thigh a rather self-conscious, gratuitous
slap. "Well, good night."

There was a chorus of "Good night, sirs,"
and then the Major went out, too, trailed by
O'Leary. Culver looked at his watch: it was
nearly three o'clock.

Mannix looked up. "You going to try and
get some sleep, Tom?"

"I've tried. It's too cold. Anyway, I've
got to take over the radio watch from Junior
here. What's your name, fellow?"

The boy at the radio looked up with a
start, trembling with the cold. "McDonald,
sir." He was very young, with pimples and a
sweet earnest expression; he had obviously
just come from boot camp, for he had practically no hair.

"Well, you can shove off and get some sleep, if you can find a nice warm pile of pine needles somewhere." The boy sleepily put down his earphones and went out, fastening the blackout flap behind him.

"I've tried," Culver repeated, "but I just can't get used to sleeping on the ground any more. I'm getting old and rheumatic. Anyway, the Old Rock was in here for about two hours before you came, using up my sack time while he told the Major and O'Leary and me all about his Shanghai days."

"He's a son of a bitch." Mannix morosely cupped his chin in his hands, blinking into space, at the bare canvas wall. He was chewing on the butt of a cigar. The glare seemed to accentuate a flat Mongoloid cast in his face; he looked surly and tough and utterly exhausted. Shivering, he pulled his field jacket closer around his neck, and then, as Culver watched, his face broke out into the comical, exasperated smile which always heralded his bitterest moments of outrage —at the Marine Corps, at the system, at their helpless plight, the state of the world—tirades which, in their unqualified cynicism,

would have been intolerable were they not always delivered with such gusto and humor
and a kind of grisly delight. "Thirty . . .
six . . . *miles*," he said slowly, his eyes alive
and glistening, *"thirty . . . six . . . miles!*
Christ on a crutch! Do you realize how far
that is? Why that's as far as it is from Grand
Central to Stamford, Connecticut! Why, man,
I haven't walked a hundred consecutive yards
since 1945. I couldn't go thirty-six miles if I
were sliding downhill the whole way on a
sled. And a *forced* march, mind you. You
just don't stroll along, you know. That's like
running. That's a regulation two-and-a-half
miles per hour with only a ten-minute break
each hour. So H & S Company is fouled
up. So maybe it is. He can't take green troops
like these and do that. After a couple of
seven- or ten- or fifteen-mile conditioning
hikes, maybe so. If they were young. And
rested. Barracks-fresh. But this silly son of a
bitch is going to have all these tired, flabby
old men flapping around on the ground like a
bunch of fish after the first two miles. Christ
on a frigging crutch!"

"He's not a bad guy, Al," Culver said,

"he's just a regular. Shot in the ass with the Corps. A bit off his nut, like all of them."

But Mannix had made the march seem menacing, there was no doubt about that, and Culver—who for the moment had been regarding the hike as a sort of careless abstraction, a prolonged evening's stroll—felt a solid dread creep into his bones, along with the chill of the night. Involuntarily, he shuddered. He felt suddenly unreal and disoriented, as if through some curious second sight or seventh sense his surroundings had shifted, ever so imperceptibly, into another dimension of space and time. Perhaps he was just so tired. Freezing marsh and grass instead of wood beneath his feet, the preposterous cold in the midst of summer, Mannix's huge distorted shadow cast brutishly against the impermeable walls by a lantern so sinister that its raging noise had the sound of a typhoon at sea—all these, just for an instant, did indeed contrive to make him feel as if they were adrift at sea in a dazzling, windowless box, ignorant of direction or of any points of the globe, and with no way of telling. What he had had for the last years—wife and child and home—seemed to have existed in the infinite past or, dreamlike again, never at all, and what he had done yesterday and the day before, moving wearily with this tent from one strange thicket to a stranger swamp and on to the green depths of some even stranger ravine, had no sequence, like the dream of a man delirious with fever. All time and space seemed for a moment to be enclosed within the tent, itself unmoored and unhelmed upon a dark and compassless ocean.

And although Mannix was close by, he felt profoundly alone. Something that had happened that evening—something Mannix had said, or suggested, perhaps not even that, but only a fleeting look in the Captain's face, the old compressed look of torment mingled with seething outrage—something that evening, without a doubt, had added to the great load of his loneliness an almost intolerable burden. And that burden was simply an anxiety, nameless for the moment and therefore the more menacing. It was not merely the prospect of the hike. Exhaustion had just made him vulnerable to a million shaky, anony-

mous fears—fears which he might have re-
sisted had he felt strong and refreshed, or
younger. His age was showing badly. All this
would have been easy at twenty-three. But he
was thirty, and seventy-two virtually sleepless
hours had left him feeling bushed and de-
feated. And there was another subtle difference he felt about his advanced age—a new
awakening, an awareness—and therein lay
the reason for his fears.

It was simply that after six years of an
ordered and sympathetic life—made the
more placid by the fact that he had assumed
he had put war forever behind him—it was a
shock almost mystically horrifying, in its unreality, to find himself in this new world of
frigid nights and blazing noons, of disorder
and movement and fanciful pursuit. He was
insecure and uprooted and the prey of many
fears. Not for days but for weeks, it seemed,
the battalion had been on the trail of an in-
visible enemy who always eluded them and
kept them pressing on—across swamps and
blasted fields and past indolent, alien
streams. This enemy was labeled Aggressor,
on maps brightly spattered with arrows and

symbolic tanks and guns, but although there
was no sign of his aggression he fled them
nonetheless and they pushed the sinister
chase, sending up shells and flares as they
went. Five hours' pause, five hours in a tent
somewhere, lent to the surrounding grove of
trees a warm, homelike familiarity that was
almost like permanence, and he left each
command post feeling lonely and uprooted,
as they pushed on after the spectral foe into
the infinite strangeness of another swamp or
grove. Fatigue pressed down on his shoulders like strong hands, and he awoke in the
morning feeling weary, if he ever slept at all.
Since their constant movement made the sunlight come from ever-shifting points of the
compass, he was often never quite sure—in
his steady exhaustion—whether it was morning or afternoon. The displacement and the
confusion filled him with an anxiety which
would not have been possible six years before, and increased his fatigue. The tent itself, in its tiny, momentary permanence,
might have had all of the appeal of the home
which he so desperately hungered for, had it
not been so cold, and had it not seemed, as he

sat there suddenly shivering with fear, so much more like a coffin instead.

Then it occurred to him that he was actually terrified of the march, of the thirty-six miles: not because of the length—which was beyond comprehension—but because he was sure he'd not be able to make it. The contagion of Mannix's fear had touched him. And he wondered then if Mannix's fear had been like his own: that no matter what his hatred of the system, of the Marine Corps, might be, some instilled, twisted pride would make him walk until he dropped, and his fear was not of the hike itself, but of dropping. He looked up at Mannix and said, "Do you think you can make it, Al?"

Mannix heavily slapped his knee. He seemed not to have heard the question. The giddy sensation passed, and Culver got up to warm his hands at the lamp.

"I'll bet if Regiment or Division got wind of this they'd lower the boom on the bastard," Mannix said.

"They have already. They said fine."

"What do you mean? How do you know?"

"He said so, before you came in. He radioed to the base for permission, or so he said."

"The bastard."

"He wouldn't dare without it," Culver said. "What I can't figure out is why Regiment gave him the O.K. on it."

"The swine. The little swine. It's not on account of H & S Company. You know that. It's because it's an exploit. He wants to be known as a tough guy, a boondocker."

"There's one consolation, though," said Culver, after a pause, "if it'll help you any."

"What, for God's sake?"

"Old Rocky, or whatever they call him, is going to hike along, too."

"You think so?" Mannix said doubtfully.

"I know so. So do you. He wouldn't dare not push along with his men."

Mannix was silent for a moment. Then he said viciously, as if obsessed with the idea that no act of Templeton's could remain untainted by a prime and calculated evil: "But the son of a bitch! He's made for that sort of thing. He's been running around the boondocks for six years getting in shape while sane people like you and me were home living like humans and taking it easy. Billy

Lawrence, too. They're both gung ho. These fat civilians can't take that sort of thing. My God! Hobbs! Look at that radioman, Hobbs. That guy's going to keel over two minutes out—" He rose suddenly to his feet and stretched, his voice stifled by the long, indrawn breath of a yawn. "Aaa-h, fuck it. I'm going to hit the sack."

"Why don't you?"

"Fine bed. A poncho in a pile of poison ivy. My ass looks like a chessboard from chigger bites. Jesus, if Mimi could see me now." He paused and pawed at his red-rimmed eyes. "Yeah," he said, blinking at his watch, "I think I will." He slapped Culver on the back, without much heartiness. "I'll see you tomorrow, sport. Stay loose." Then he lumbered from the tent, mumbling something: *be in for fifty years.*

Culver turned away from the lamp. He sat down at the field desk, strapping a black garland of wires and earphones around his skull. The wild, lost wail of the radio signal struck his ears, mingling with the roar, much closer now, of the lamp; alone as he was, the chill and cramped universe of the tent seemed

made for no one more competent than a blind
midget, and was on the verge of bursting with
a swollen obbligato of demented sounds. He
felt almost sick with the need for sleep and,
with the earphones still around his head, he
thrust his face into his arms on the field desk.
There was nothing on the radio except the
signal; far off in the swamp the companies
were sleeping wretchedly in scattered squads
and platoons, tumbled about in the cold and
the dark, and dreaming fitful dreams. The
radios were dead everywhere, except for their
signals: a crazy, tortured multitude of wails
on which his imagination played in exhaustion. They seemed like the cries of souls in
the anguish of hell, if he concentrated closely
enough, shrill cracklings, whines, barks and
shrieks—a whole jungle full of noise an inch
from his eardrum and across which, like a
thread of insanity, was strung the single faint
fluting of a dance-band clarinet—blown in
from Florida or New York, someplace beyond reckoning. His universe now seemed
even more contained: not merely by the tiny
space of the tent, but by the almost tangible
fact of sound. And it was impossible to sleep.

Besides, something weighed heavily on his mind; there was something he had forgotten, something he was supposed to do . . .

Then suddenly he remembered the Colonel's instructions. He cleared his throat and spoke drowsily into the mouthpiece, his head still resting against his arms. "This is Bundle Three calling Bundle Able. This is Bundle Three calling Bundle Able. This is Bundle Three calling Bundle Able. Do you hear me? Over . . ." He paused for a moment, waiting. There was no answer. He repeated: "This is Bundle Three calling Bundle Able, this is Bundle Three calling Bundle Able, this is. . . ." And he snapped abruptly erect, thinking of Mannix, thinking: to hell with it: simply because the words made him feel juvenile and absurd, as if he were reciting Mother Goose.

He *would* stay awake. And he thought of Mannix. Because Mannix would laugh. Mannix appreciated the idiocy of those radio words, just as in his own crazy way he managed to put his finger on anything which might represent a symbol of their predicament. Like the radio code. He had a violent contempt for the gibberish, the boy-scout passwords which replaced ordinary conversation in the military world. To Mannix they were all part of the secret language of a group of morons, morons who had been made irresponsibly and dangerously clever. He had despised the other side, also—the sweat, the exertion, and the final danger. It had been he, too, who had said, "None of this Hemingway crap for me, Jack"; he was nobody's lousy hero, and he'd get out of this outfit some way. Yet, Culver speculated, who really was a hero anyway, any more? Mannix's disavowal of faith put him automatically out of the hero category, in the classical sense, yet if suffering was part of the hero's role, wasn't Mannix as heroic as any? On his shoulder there was a raw, deeply dented, livid scar, made the more conspicuous and, for that matter, more ugly, by the fact that its evil slick surface only emphasized the burly growth of hair around it. There were smaller scars all over his body. About them Mannix was neither proud nor modest, but just frank, and once while they were showering down after a day in the field, Mannix told him how he had gotten the scars, one day on Peleliu. "I was a buck sergeant then. I got pinned down in a shell hole out in front of my platoon. Christ knows how I got there but I remember there was a telephone in the hole and—whammo! —the Nips began laying in mortar fire on the area and I got a piece right here." He pointed to a shiny, triangular groove just above his knee. "I remember grabbing that phone and hollering for them to for Christ's sake get the 81s up and knock out that position, but they were slow, Jesus they were slow! The Nips were firing for effect, I guess, because they were coming down like rain and every time one of the goddam things went off I seemed to catch it. All I can remember is hollering into that phone and the rounds go-ing off and the zinging noise that shrapnel made. I hollered for 81s and I caught a piece in my hand. Then I hollered for at least a goddam rifle grenade and I caught a piece in the ass, right here. I hollered for 60s and guns and airplanes. Every time I hollered for something I seemed to catch some steel. Christ, I was scared. And hurting! Jesus Christ, I never hurt so much in my life. Then

I caught this one right here"—he made a comical, contorted gesture, with a bar of soap, over his shoulder—"man, it was lights out then. I remember thinking, 'Al, you've had it,' and just before I passed out I looked down at that telephone. You know, that frigging wire had been blasted right out of sight all that time."

No, perhaps Mannix wasn't a hero, any more than the rest of them, caught up by wars in which, decade by half-decade, the combatant served peonage to the telephone and the radar and the thunderjet—a horde of cunningly designed, and therefore often treacherous, machines. But Mannix had suffered once, that "once" being, in his own words, "once too goddam many, Jack." And his own particular suffering had made him angry, had given him an acute, if cynical, perception about their renewed bondage, and a keen nose for the winds that threatened to blow up out of the oppressive weather of their surroundings and sweep them all into violence. And he made Culver uneasy. His discontent was not merely peevish; it was rocklike and rebellious, and thus this discontent seemed to Culver to be at once brave and somehow full of peril.

He had first seen Mannix the revolutionary five months ago, soon after they had been called back to duty. He hadn't known him then. There were compulsory lectures arranged at first, to acquaint the junior officers with recent developments in what had been called "the new amphibious doctrine." The outlines of these lectures were appallingly familiar: the stuffy auditorium asprawl with bored lieutenants and captains, the brightly lit stage with its magnified charts and graphs, the lantern slides (at which point, when the lights went out, it was possible to sneak a moment's nap, just as in officers' school seven years ago), the parade of majors and colonels with their maps and pointers, and their cruelly tedious, doggedly memorized lectures: the whole scene, with its grave, professorial air, seemed seedily portentous, especially since no one cared, save the majors and colonels, and no one listened. When Culver sat down, during the darkness of a lantern slide, next to the big relaxed mass which he dimly identified as a captain, he noticed that it was

snoring. When the lights went up, Mannix
still slept on, filling the air around him with
a loud, tranquil blubber. Culver aroused him
with a nudge. Mannix grumbled something,
but then said, "Thanks, Jack." A young colonel had come onto the stage then. He had
made many of the lectures that week. He
had a curiously thick, throaty voice which
would have made him sound like a yokel, except that his words were coolly, almost pas-
sionately put, and he bent forward over the
lectern with a bleak and solemn attitude—a
lean, natty figure with hair cut so close to his
head that he appeared to be, from that distance, nearly bald. "An SS man," Mannix
whispered, "he's gonna come down here and
cut your balls off. You Jewish?" He grinned
and collapsed back, forehead against his
hand, into quiet slumber. Culver couldn't recall what the colonel talked about: the movement of supplies, logistics, ship-to-shore
movement, long-range planning, all abstract
and vast, and an ardent glint came to his eyes
when he spoke of the "grandiose doctrine"
which had been formulated since they, the
reserves, had been away. "You bet your life,

Jack," Mannix had whispered out of the shadows then. He seemed to have snapped fully awake and, following the lecture intently, he appeared to address his whispers not to Culver, or the colonel, but to the air. "You bet your life they're grandiose," he said, "even if you don't know what grandiose means. I'll bet you'd sell your soul to be able to drop a bomb on somebody." And then, aping the colonel's instructions to the corporal—one of the enlisted flunkies who, after each lecture, passed out the reams of printed and mimeographed tables and charts and résumés, which everyone promptly, when out of sight, threw away—he whispered in high, throaty, lilting mockery: "Corporal, kindly pass out the atom bombs for inspection." He smacked the arm of his seat, too hard; it could be heard across the auditorium, and heads turned then, but the colonel had not seemed to have noticed. "Jesus," Mannix rumbled furiously, "Jesus Christ almighty," while the colonel droned on, in his countrified voice: "Our group destiny," he said, "amphibiously integrated, from any force thrown against us by Aggressor enemy."

Later—toward the end of that week of lectures, after Mannix had spoken the calm, public manifesto which at least among the reserves had made him famous, and from then on the object of a certain awe, though with a few doubts about his balance, too—Culver had tried to calculate how he had gotten by with it. Perhaps it had to do with his size, his bearing. There was at times a great massive absoluteness in the way he spoke. He was huge, and the complete honesty and candor of his approach seemed to rumble forth, like notes from a sounding board, in direct proportion to his size. He had suffered, too, and this suffering had left a persistent, unwhipped, scornful look in his eyes, almost like a stain, or rather a wound, which spells out its own warning and cautions the unwary to handle this tortured parcel of flesh with care. And he was an enormous man, his carriage was formidable. That skinny, bristle-haired colonel, Culver finally realized, had been taken aback past the point of punishment, or even reprimand, merely because of the towering, unavoidable, physical fact that he was facing not a student or a captain or a subordinate, but a stubborn and passionate man. So it was that, after a lecture on transport of supplies, when the colonel had called Mannix's name at random from a list to answer some generalized, hypothetical question, Mannix had stood up and said merely, "I don't know, sir." A murmur of surprise passed over the auditorium then, for the colonel, early in the hour, had made it plain that he had wanted at least an attempt at an answer—a guess—even though they might be unacquainted with the subject. But Mannix merely said, "I don't know, sir," while the colonel, as if he hadn't heard correctly, rephrased the question with a little tremor of annoyance. There was a moment's silence and men turned around in their seats to look at the author of this defiance. "I don't know, sir," he said again, in a loud but calm voice. "I don't know what my first consideration would be in making a space table like that. I'm an infantry officer. I got an 0302." The colonel's forehead went pink under the glare of the lights. "I stated earlier, Captain, that I wanted some sort of answer. None of you gentlemen is expected to know this subject pat, but you can essay *some kind of an answer*." Mannix just stood there, solid and huge, blinking at the colonel. "I just have to repeat, sir," he said finally, "that I don't have the faintest idea what my first consideration would be. I never went to cargo-loading school. I'm an 0302. And I'd like to respectfully add, sir, if I might, that there's hardly anybody in this room who knows that answer, either. They've forgotten everything they ever learned seven years ago. Most of them don't even know how to take an M-1 apart. They're too old. They should be home with their family." There was passion in his tone but it was controlled and straightforward—he had managed to keep out of his voice either anger or insolence—and then he fell silent. His words had the quality, the sternness, of an absolute and unequivocal fact, as if they had been some intercession for grace spoken across the heads of a courtroom by a lawyer so quietly convinced of his man's innocence that there was no need for gesticulations or frenzy. The colonel's eyes bulged incredulously at Mannix from across the rows of seats, but in the complete, astounded hush that had followed

he was apparently at a loss for words. A bit
unsteadily, he called out another name and
Mannix sat down, staring stonily ahead.

It had been perhaps a court-martial offense, at least worthy of some reprimand, but
that was all there was to it. Nothing happened, no repercussions, nothing. The thing
had been forgotten; either that, or it had
been stored away in the universal memory of
colonels, where all such incidents are sorted
out for retribution, or are forgotten. Whatever effect it had on the colonel, or whatever
higher, even more important sources got
wind of it, it had its effect on Mannix. And
the result was odd. Far from giving the impression that he had been purged, that he had
blown off excess pressure, he seemed instead
more tense, more embittered, more in need to
scourge something—his own boiling spirit,
authority, anything.

Culver's vision of him at this time was always projected against Heaven's Gate, which
was the name—no doubt ironically supplied
at first by the enlisted men—of the pleasure-
dome ingeniously erected amid a tangle of
alluvial swampland, and for officers only. He

and Mannix lived in rooms next to each other, in the bachelor quarters upstairs. The entire area was a playground which had all the casual opulence of a Riviera resort and found its focus in the sparkling waters of a swimming pool, set like an oblong sapphire amid flowered walks and a fanciful growth of beach umbrellas. There, at ten minutes past four each day, Mannix could be found, his uniform shed in an instant and a gin fizz in his hand—a sullen, mountainous figure in a lurid sportshirt, across which a squadron of monstrous butterflies floated in luminous, un-military files. Both Mannix and Culver hated the place—its factitious luxury, its wanton atmosphere of alcohol and torpid ease and dances, the vacant professional talk of the regular officers and the constant teasing pres-ence of their wives, who were beautiful and spoke in tender drawls and boldly flaunted at the wifeless reserves—in a proprietary, At-lanta-debutante fashion—their lecherous sort of chastity. The place seemed to offer up, like a cornucopia, the fruits of boredom, of foot-lessness and dissolution. It was, in Mannix's words, like a prison where you could have anything you wanted except happiness, and once, in a rare midnight moment when he allowed himself to get drunk, he got paper and wood together from his room and announced to Culver in an unsteady but determined voice that he was going to burn the place down. Culver held him off, but it was true: they were bound to the pleasures of the place by necessity—for there was no place to go for a hundred miles, even if they had wanted to go —and therefore out of futility. "Goddam, it's degrading," Mannix had said, making use of an adjective which indeed seemed to sum it all up. "It's like sex now. Or the lack of it. Now maybe it's all right for a kid to go without sex, but it's degrading for someone like me almost thirty to go without making love for so long. It's simply degrading, that's all. I'd go for one of these regulars' pigs if it wasn't for Mimi. . . . This whole mess is degrading. I know it's my own fault I stayed in the reserves, Jack, you don't have to tell me that. I was a nut. I didn't know I was going to get called out for every frigging international incident that came along. But, goddam, it's degrading"—and with a glum, subdued

gesture he'd down the dregs of his drink—
"it's degrading for a man my age to go
sniffing around on my belly in the boondocks
like a dog. And furthermore—" He looked
scornfully about him, at the glitter and
chrome, at the terrace by the pool where Japa-
nese lanterns hung like a grove of pastel
moons, and a girl's shrill and empty laugh
uncoiled as bright as tinsel through the slug-
gish coastal dusk. It was a silent moment in a
night sprinkled with a dusty multitude of
Southern stars, and the distant bleating saxo-
phone seemed indecisive and sad, like the
nation and the suffocating summer, neither at
peace nor at war. "Furthermore, it's degrading to come out of the field each day and then
be *forced* to go to a night club like this, when
all you want to do is go home to your wife
and family. Goddam, man, I've *gotta* get
out!"

But underneath his rebellion, Culver
finally knew, Mannix—like all of them—was
really resigned. Born into a generation of
conformists, even Mannix (so Culver sensed)
was aware that his gestures were not symbolic, but individual, therefore hopeless,

maybe even absurd, and that he was trapped like all of them in a predicament which one personal insurrection could, if anything, only make worse. "You know," he said once, "I think I was really afraid just one time last war." The phrase "last war" had had, itself, a numb, resigned quality, in its lack of any particular inflection, like "last week end," or "last movie I went to see." They had been lying on the beach to which they fled each hot week end. In that setting of coast and sea and lugubrious solitude they felt nearly peaceful, in touch with a tranquil force more important, and more lasting (or so it seemed on those sunlit afternoons), than war. Mannix had been, almost for the first time since Culver had known him, rested and subdued, and the sound of his voice had been a surprise after long, sun-laden hours of sleep and silence. "That's the goddam truth," he said thoughtfully, "I was only afraid once. Really afraid, I mean. It was at a hotel in San Francisco. I think I really came closer to dying that night than I ever have in my life. We were drunk, you see, polluted, all of us. I think there were five of us, all of us boots just out of Dago. Kids. We were on the tenth floor of this hotel and in this room and I believe we were about as drunk as anyone could get. I remember going in to take a shower in the bathroom. It was late at night, past midnight, and after I took this shower, you see, I came out into the room buck naked. Two of those drunk guys were waiting for me. They grabbed me and pushed me toward the window. I was so loaded I couldn't battle. Then they pushed me out the window and held me by the heels while I dangled upside-down buck naked in space, ten floors above the street." He paused and sucked at a beer can. "Can you imagine that?" he went on slowly. "How I felt? I got stone-sober in a second. Imagine being that high upside-down in space with two drunks holding onto your heels. I was heavy, man, just like now, you see. All I can remember is those teeny-weeny lights below and the tiny little people like ants down there and those two crazy drunk guys holding onto my wet slippery ankles, laughing like hell and trying to decide whether to let go or not. I just remember the cold wind blowing on my body and that dark, man, infinite darkness all around me, and my ankles beginning to slip out of their hands. I really saw Death then, and I think that all I could think of was that I was going to fall and smash myself on that hard, hard street below. That those crazy bastards were going to let me fall. I was praying, I guess. I remember the blood rushing to my brain and my ankles slipping, and that awful strange noise. And I was reaching out, man, clutching at thin air. Then I wondered what that noise was, that high loud noise, and then I realized it was me, screaming at the top of my voice, all over San Francisco." He stopped talking then and scuffed at the sand with one calloused heel. "They hauled me up somehow. It was those sober guys—I guess they were sober—the other two. They got me up. But every time I remember that moment a great big cold shudder runs up and down my spine." He chuckled and chewed on his cigar but the laugh was half-hearted and listless, and he dug his elbows into the sand and resumed his quiet, placid gaze toward the horizon. Culver watched him: his bitterness dissolved in the hot salty air, slumped in the sand gazing wistfully out to sea, sun-glassed, hairy-chested, a cigar protruding from his face and a beer can warming in his hand, he seemed no longer the man who could sicken himself with resentment, but relaxed, pliable even, like a huge hairy baby soothed by the wash of elemental tides, ready to receive anything, all, into that great void in his soul which bitterness and rebellion had briefly left vacant—all—the finality of more suffering, or even death. War was in the offing. A promenade of waves, snow-crowned like lovely garlands in the dark hair of girls, swelled eastward toward Africa: past those smoky heights, more eastward still, the horizon seemed to give back repeated echoes of the sea, like far-off thunder, or guns. Culver remembered making a quick, contorted motion in the sand with his body, and being swept by a hot wave of anguish. It was loneliness and homesickness, but it was also fright. Across the rim of his memory two little girls playing on the sunny grass waved to him, were gone, pursued by a shower of uncapturable musical sounds. Mannix's resigned silence fed his loneliness. Suddenly he felt, like Mannix, upturned drunkenly above the abyss, blood rushing to his head, in terror clutching at the substanceless night. . . .

In the noonday light Sergeant O'Leary, his face brightly pink, was still talking. Culver snapped awake with a start. O'Leary grinned down at him—"Damn, Lieutenant, you're gonna crap out tonight if you're that tired now"—and Culver struggled for speech; time seemed to have unspooled past him in a great spiral, and for an instant—his mind still grappling with the memory of a hurried, chaotic nightmare—he was unable to tell where he was. He had the feeling that it should be the night before, and that he was still in the tent. "Did I go to sleep, O'Leary?" he said, blinking upward.

"Yes, sir," O'Leary said, and chuckled, "you sure did."

"How long?"

"Oh, just a second."

"Christ, I *am* tired. I dreamt it was last night," Culver said. He got to his feet. A truck moved through the clearing in a cloud of dust. There seemed to be new activity in the command post, and new confusion. Culver and O'Leary turned together then toward the operations tent; the Colonel had come out and was striding toward them, followed by Mannix.

"Culver, get your jeep and driver," he said, walking toward the road, not looking up. His voice was briskly matter-of-fact; he strode past them with short, choppy steps and the swagger stick in his hand made a quick tattoo, *slap-slap*-slapping against his dungaree pants. "I want you and Captain Mannix to go with me down to Third Batt. See if we can help." His voice faded; Mannix trailed behind him, saying nothing, but his face seemed to Culver even more exhausted, and even more grimly taut, than it had been an hour before.

The road was a dusty cart-path that rambled footlessly across scrubby, fallow farmland. Shacks and cabins, long ago abandoned, lay along its way. They piled into the jeep, Mannix and Culver in the back, the Colonel in front next to the driver. They hadn't far to go—less than a mile—but the trip felt endless to Culver because the day, by now a fit-

ful carrousel of sleepy sounds, motions without meaning, seemed wildly, almost dangerously abstracted, as if viewed through
drug-glazed eyes or eyes, like those of a mole,
unacquainted with light. Dust billowed past
them as they went. Above them a blue cloud-
less sky in which the sun, pitched now at its
summit, beat fearfully down, augured no
rain for the day, or for the evening. Mannix
said nothing; his silence prompted Culver to
turn and look at him. He was gazing straight
ahead with eyes that seemed to bore through
the Colonel's neck. Tormented beast in the
cul-de-sac, baffled fury, grief at the edge
of defeat—his eyes made Culver suddenly
aware of what they were about to see, and he
turned dizzily away and watched the wreck
of a Negro cabin float past through the
swirling dust: shell-shattered doors and sag-
ging walls, blasted façade—a target across
which for one split second in the fantastic
noon there seemed to crawl the ghosts of the
bereaved and the departed, mourning wraiths
come back to reclaim from the ruins some
hot scent of honeysuckle, smell of cooking,
murmurous noise of bees. Culver closed his

eyes and drowsed, slack-jawed, limp, his stomach faintly heaving.

One boy's eyes lay gently closed, and his long dark lashes were washed in tears, as though he had cried himself to sleep. As they bent over him they saw that he was very young, and a breeze came up from the edges of the swamp, bearing with it a scorched odor of smoke and powder, and touched the edges of his hair. A lock fell across his brow with a sort of gawky, tousled grace, as if preserving even in that blank and mindless repose some gesture proper to his years, a callow charm. Around his curly head grasshoppers darted among the weeds. Below, beneath the slumbering eyes, his face had been blasted out of sight. Culver looked up and met Mannix's gaze. The Captain was sobbing helplessly. He cast an agonized look toward the Colonel, standing across the field, then down again at the boy, then at Culver. "Won't they ever let us alone, the sons of bitches," he murmured, weeping. "Won't they ever let us alone?"

III

That evening at twilight, just before the beginning of the march, Mannix found a nail in his shoe. "Look at it," he said to Culver, "what lousy luck." They were sitting on an embankment bordering the road. The blue dusk was already scattered with stars, but evening had brought no relief to the heat of the day. It clung to them still, damp and stifling, enveloping them like an overcoat. The battalion, over a thousand men, was ready for the march. It stretched out in two files on either side of the road below them for more than a mile. Culver turned and looked down into Mannix's shoe: sure enough, a nail-end had penetrated the lining at the base of the heel, a sharp pinpoint of torture. Mannix inspected the bottom of his big dirty foot. He pulled off a flake of skin which the nail had already worn away. "Of all the lousy luck," he said, "gimme a band-aid."

"It'll wear right through, Al," Culver said, "you'd better get another pair of shoes. Try flattening it out with the end of your bayonet."

Mannix hammered for a moment at the nail and then looked up in exasperation. "It won't go all the way. Gimme that band-aid." A rusty spatter of blood he had picked up at noon was still on the sleeve of his dungarees. He had become nervous and touchy. All that afternoon, after they had come back, he had seemed, like Culver, still shaken by the slaughter, still awed, and rather despondent. Finally, he had alternated moments of remote abstraction with quick outbursts of temper. The shock of the explosion seemed to have set something off in him. His mood had become vague and unpredictable, and he was able to shift from sour, uncommunicative gloom to violent anger in an instant. Culver had never seen him quite so cranky before, nor had he ever seen him so testily at odds with his men, to whom he usually had shown the breeziest good will. All afternoon he'd been after them, nagging, bellowing orders—only to fall suddenly into a profound and brooding silence. As he squatted in the weeds eating his evening meal two hours before, he had hardly said a word, except to murmur—irrelevantly, Culver thought—that his company "had better god-dam well shape up." It puzzled Culver; the explosion seemed to have stripped off layers of skin from the Captain, leaving only raw nerves exposed.

Now he had become fretful again, touchily alert, and his voice was heavy with impatience. He mumbled as he plastered the band-aid on his foot. "I wish they'd get this show on the road. That's the trouble with the Marine Corps, you always stand frigging around for half the night while they think up some grandiose doctrine. I wish to Christ I'd joined the Army. Man, if I'd have known what I was getting in for when I went down to that recruiting office in 1941, I'd have run off at the door." He looked up from his foot and down toward the command group nearly at the head of the column. Three or four officers were clustered together on the road. The Colonel was among them, neat, almost jaunty, in new dungarees and boots. On his head there was a freshly clean utility cap with a spruce uptilted bill and a shiny little silver leaf. At his side he wore a pearl-handled .38 revolver, glistening with silver inlay. It was, as usual, loaded, though no one knew why, for he was never known to shoot it; the general feeling seemed to be that it was his emblematic prerogative, no more an affectation, certainly, than a visored hat encrusted with gilt, or grenades worn at the shoulder. The pistol—like the swagger stick; the nickname; the quizzical, almost tenderly contemplative air of authority—was part of the act, and to be sure, Culver reflected, the act was less offensive, less imperious than it might be. One simply learned soon to believe that the pistol "belonged," just as the name "Old Rocky" belonged; if such an act finally did no harm, if it only flattered his vanity, was the Colonel to be blamed, Culver asked himself, if he did nothing to mitigate the total impression?

Mannix watched him, too, watched the Colonel toe at the sand, thumbs hooked rakishly in his belt, a thin gentle smile on his face, adumbrated by the fading light: he looked youthful and fresh, nonchalant, displaying the studied casualness of an athlete before the stadium throng, confident of his own victory long before the race begins. Mannix gnawed at the end of a cigar, spat it out viciously. "Look at the little jerk. He thinks he's gonna have us pooped out at the halfway mark—"

Culver put in, "Look Al, why don't you do something about that nail? If you told the Colonel he'd let you ride in—"

Mannix went fiercely on, in a husky whisper: "Well he's not. He's a little sadist, but he's not gonna have Al Mannix crapped out. I'll walk anywhere that son of a bitch goes and a mile further. He thinks H & S Company's been doping off. Well, I'll show him. I wouldn't ask him to ride in if I'd been walking over broken glass. I'll—"

He paused. Culver turned and looked at him. They were both silent, staring at each other, embarrassed by the common understanding of their gaze. Each turned away; Mannix murmured something and began to tie his shoe. "You're right, Al," Culver heard himself saying. It seemed it was almost more than he could bear. Night was coming on. As in a stupor, he looked down the road at the battalion, the men lounging along the embankments with their rifles, smoking and

talking in tired, subdued voices, smoke rising
in giant blue clouds through the dusk, where
swarms of gnats rose and fell in vivacious,
panicky flight. In the swamp, frogs had begun a brainless chorale; their noise seemed
perfectly suited to his sense of complete and
final frustration. It was almost more than he
could bear. So Mannix had felt it, too: not
simply fear of suffering, nor exhaustion, nor
the lingering horror, which gripped both of
them, of that bloody wasteland in the noonday heat. But the other: the old atavism that
clutched them, the voice that commanded,
once again, *you will*. How stupid to think
they had ever made their own philosophy; it
was as puny as a house of straw, and at this
moment—by the noise in their brains of those
words, *you will*—it was being blasted to the
winds like dust. They were as helpless as children. Another war, and years beyond reckoning, had violated their minds irrevocably.
For six years they had slept a cataleptic sleep,
dreaming blissfully of peace, awakened in
horror to find that, after all, they were only
marines, responding anew to the old commands. They were marines. Even if they were

old. Bank clerks and salesmen and lawyers. Even if, right now, they were unutterably tired. They could no more *not* be determined to walk the thirty-six miles than they could, in the blink of an eye, turn themselves into beautiful nymphs. Culver was afraid he wasn't going to make it, and now he knew Mannix was afraid, and he didn't know what to feel—resentment or disgust—over the fact that his fear was mingled with a faint, fugitive pride.

Mannix looked up from his shoe and at the Colonel. "You're goddam right, Jack, we're going to make it," he said. "My company's going to make it if I have to *drag in their bodies*." There was a tone in his voice that Culver had never heard before.

Suddenly the Colonel's flat voice broke through the stillness: "All right, Billy, let's saddle up."

" 'Tallion saddle up!" The Major's words were eager and shrill, became multiplied down the long mile. "Smoking lamp's out!" The blue cloud dissolved on the air, the gnats descended in a swarm and the voices passed on—*Saddle up, saddle up*—while the bat-

talion rose to its feet, not all at once but in a
steady gradual surge, like rows of corn snap-
ping back erect after the passing of a wind.
Mannix got to his feet, began to sideslip in
a cloud of dust down the embankment toward
his company directly below. It was at the
head of the column, right behind the command group. Culver, moving himself now
down the hill, heard Mannix's shout. It rang
out in the dusk with deliberate authority,
hoarse blunt command: "All right, H & S
Company, saddle up, saddle up! You people
get off your asses and straighten up!" Culver
passed by him on his way to the command
group: he stood surrounded by a cloud of
gnats, hulking enormously above the company, hands balanced lightly on his hips,
poised forward badgering the men like some
obsessed, rakehell Civil War general before a
battle: "All right, you people, we're gonna
walk thirty-six miles tonight and I mean
walk! First man I see drop out's gonna get
police duty for two weeks, and that goes for
everybody. You think I'm kidding you wait
and see. There's gonna be trucks going in for
those that can't make it but I don't want to

see anyone from H & S Company climbing on!
If an old man with as much flab as I've got
can make it you people can too . . ." There
was a note, almost, of desperation in his
voice. Culver, passing along the line of bedraggled, mournful-looking men, so few of
whom looked like fabled marines, heard the
voice rise to a taut pitch close to frenzy; it
was too loud, it worried Culver, and he
wished to caution him: no longer just ad-
monishing the men to a simple duty, it was the
voice of a man wildly fanatic with one idea:
to last. "I want to hear no bitching out of you
people! Take it easy on the water. You get
shinsplints or blisters you see the corpsman, don't come crying to me. When we get
in I want to see all of you people . . ." Not
because the hike was good or even sensible,
Culver thought, but out of hope of triumph,
like a chain-gang convict who endures a flog-
ging without the slightest whimper, only to
spite the flogger. Culver joined the command
group, heard the Colonel say to the Major:
"Looks like H & S Company's going to make
it *en masse*, Billy." It was just as Culver
feared, for although his words were pleasant

enough, his face, regarding Mannix for a brief moment, had a look of narrow scrutiny, as if he, too, had detected in the Captain's tone that note of proud and willful submission, rebellion in reverse. But there was no emotion in his voice as he turned quickly, with a glance at his watch, and said, "Let's move out, Billy."

They started out without delay. A jeep, its headlamps lit, preceded them. The Colonel, in the lead, abreast of the Major and just ahead of Culver, plunged off into the deep dust of the road. He walked with a slinky-hipped, athletic stride, head down between his shoulders and slightly forward, arms bent and moving methodically; nothing broke the rhythm of his steps—ruts in the road or the deeply grooved tire tracks—and Culver became quickly amazed, and rather appalled, at the pace he was setting. It was the pace of a trained hiker—determined, unhesitant, much closer to a trot now than a walk—and only a few minutes passed before Culver was gasping for breath. Sand lay thick in the road, hindering a natural step. They had not gone more than a couple of hundred yards; already he felt sweat trickling down his forehead and beneath his arms. For a moment fear surged up in him unnaturally, and a crazy panic. He had been afraid of the march before, but his fear had been abstract and hazy; now so quickly fatigued, in what seemed a matter of seconds, he felt surely (as Mannix had predicted) that he'd be unable to last the first hour. A panicky wash of blood came to his face and he struggled for breath, wanting to cry out—it passed. His mind groped for reason and the terror receded: once he adjusted to the shock of this pace, he realized, he'd be all right. Then the panic went away; as it did so, he found himself breathing easier, freed of that irrational fright. The Colonel pushed ahead in front of him with the absolute mechanical confidence of a wound-up, strutting tin soldier on a table top. Culver, panting a bit, heard his voice, as calm and unwinded as if he were sitting at a desk somewhere, addressed to the Major: "We shoved off at nine on the dot, Billy. We should make the main road at ten and have a break." "Yes, sir," he heard the Major say, "we'll be ahead of the game." Culver made a calculation then;

by the operations map, which he knew so
well, that was three and a half miles—a mile
farther than the regulation distance for an
hour's march. It was, indeed, like running.
Pushing on through the sand, he felt a wave
of hopelessness so giddy and so incompre-
hensible that it was almost like exhilaration
—and he heard a noise—half-chuckle, half-
groan—escape between his labored breaths.
Three and a half miles: the distance from
Greenwich Village almost to Harlem. In his
mind he measured that giddy parade of city
blocks, an exhausting voyage even on wheels.
It was like twisting a knife in his side but he
went on with the mental yardstick—to imagine himself plodding that stretch up the
sandless, comfortably receptive pavements of
Fifth Avenue, past Fourteenth Street and the
bleak vistas of the Twenties and the Thirties,
hurrying onward north by the Library, twenty
blocks more to the Plaza, and pressing still
onward along the green acres of the Park
. . . his thoughts recoiled. Three and a half
miles. In an hour. With more than thirty-
two still to go. A vision of Mannix came
swimming back; Culver stumbled along

after the dauntless Colonel, thinking, Christ
on a crutch.

They hastened on. Night had fallen around
them, tropic and sudden, lit now, as they descended across a thicket of swampy ground,
only by the lights of the jeep. Culver had re-
gained his wind but already his chest and
back were awash in sweat, and he was thirsty.
He took a vague comfort in the fact that others felt the same way, for behind him he
heard canteens being unsnapped from their
cases, rattling out of their cups, and the noise,
in mid-march, of drinking—a choked, gur-
gling sound—then, faint to the rear, Mannix's angry voice: "All right, goddammit, I
told you people to hold onto your water! Put
those goddam canteens back until the break!"
Culver, craning his neck around, saw nothing
—no Mannix, who had apparently dropped
behind—nothing except a shadowy double
line of men laboring through the sand, fading
off far down the road into the general black-
ness. To the rear some marine made a joke, a
remark; there was laughter and a snatch of
song—*on top of old Smo-oky, all covered*

. . . Then Mannix's voice again out of the dark: "O.K. you people can grabass all you want but I'm telling you you'd better save your wind. If you want to talk all the way it's O.K. with me but you're gonna crap out if you do, and remember what I said . . ." His tone had become terse and vicious; it could have been the sound of a satrap of Pharaoh, a galley master. It had the forbidding quality of a strand of barbed wire or a lash made of thorns, and the voices, the song, abruptly ceased, as if they had been strangled. Still his words continued to sting and flay them—already, in this first hour, with the merciless accents of a born bully—and Culver, suddenly angered, had an impulse to drop back and try to make him let up.

"You people close it up now! Dammit, Shea, keep those men closed up there. They fall back they're gonna have to run to catch up! Goddammit, close it up now, you hear me! I mean *you*, Thompson, goddammit you aren't deaf! Close it up! *Close it up*, I said!" So it was that the voice, brutal and furious, continued the rest of the way.

And so it was that those first hours Culver recollected as being the most harrowing of all, even though the later hours brought more subtle refinements of pain. He reasoned that this was because during the first few miles or so he was at least in rough possession of his intellect, his mind lashing his spirit as pitilessly as his body. Later, he seemed to be involved in something routine, an act in which his brain, long past cooperation, played hardly any part at all. But during these early hours there was also the fact of Mannix. Superimposed upon Culver's own fantasies, his anger, his despair (and his own calm moments of rationalization, too) was his growing awareness of what was happening to the Captain. Later, Mannix's actions seemed to become mixed up and a part of the general scheme, the nightmare. But here at first Culver's mind was enough in focus for Mannix's transformation to emerge clearly, even if with the chill, unreal outlines of coming doom—like a man conversing, who might turn around briefly to a mirror and see behind him in the room no longer his familiar friend, but something else—a shape, a ghost, a horror—a wild and threatful face reflected from the glass.

They made the highway at ten o'clock, almost to the minute. When the Colonel looked at his watch and stopped and the Major raised his arm, shouting, "Breather! Ten minutes!" Culver went over to the side of the road and sat down in the weeds. Blood was knocking angrily at his temples, behind his eyes, and he was thirsty enough to drink, with a greedy recklessness, nearly a third of his canteen. He lit a cigarette; it tasted foul and metallic and he flipped it away. His knees and thighs, unaccustomed to so much pounding, were stiff and fatigued; he stretched them out slowly into the dewy underbrush, looking upward at a placid cloud of stars. He turned. Up the road, threading its way through a barrier of outstretched legs and rifles, came a figure. It was Mannix. He was still muttering as he lumbered up and sank down beside him. "Those goddam people, they won't keep it closed up. I have to dog them every minute. They're going to find themselves running the whole way if they don't keep closed up. Gimme a butt." He was breathing heavily, and he passed the back of his hand over his brow to wipe the sweat away.

"Why don't you leave them alone?" Culver said. He gave the Captain a cigarette, which he lit, blowing the smoke out in a violent sort of choked puff.

"Dammit," he replied, coughing, "you *can't* leave them alone! They don't want to make this lousy hike. They'd just as soon crap out on the side and let the trucks haul them in. They'd just as soon take police duty. Man, they're reserves. They don't care who sees them crap out—me, anybody." He fell back with a sigh into the weeds, arms over his eyes. "Fuck it," he said. Culver looked down at him. From the jeep's headlamps an oblong of yellow slanted across the lower part of his face. One corner of his mouth jerked nervously—a distasteful grimace, as if he had been chewing something sour. Exhausted, completely bushed, there was something in his manner—even in repose—which refused to admit his own exhaustion. He clenched his teeth convulsively together. It was as if his own fury, his own obsession now, held up,

Atlas-like, the burden of his great weariness. "Jesus," he murmured, almost irrelevantly, "I can't help thinking about those kids today, lying out there in the weeds."

Culver rested easily for a moment, thinking too. He looked at his watch, with a sinking sensation: six of their ten minutes had already passed—so swiftly that they seemed not to have existed at all. Then he said, "Well, for Christ's sake, Al, why don't you let them crap out? If you were getting screwed like these enlisted men are you'd crap out too, you wouldn't care. You don't have to chew them out like you've been doing. Let's face it, you don't really care if they make it. You. Me, maybe. But these guys . . . anybody else. What the hell." He paused, fumbling for words, went on feebly, "*Do* you?"

Mannix rose up on his elbows then. "You're damn right I do," he said evenly. They turned toward the Colonel standing not far away; he and the Major, pointing a flashlight, were bent together over a map. Mannix hawked something up and spat. His voice became more controlled. "You see that little jerk standing there?" he said. "He thinks he's pulling something on us. Thirty-six miles. *No*body walks that far, stateside. *No*body. We never walked that far even with Edson, last war. See, that little jerk wants to make a name for himself—Old Rocky Templeton. Led the longest forced march in the history of the Corps—"

"But—" Culver started.

"He'd just love to see H & S Company crap out," he went on tensely, "he'd *love* it. It'd do something to his ego. Man, I can see him now"— and his voice lifted itself in a tone of sour mockery— " 'Well, Cap'n Mannix, see where you had a little trouble last night getting your men in. Need a little bit more *esprit*, huh?' " His voice lowered, filled with venom. "Well, screw *him*, Jack. I'll get my company in if I have to carry them on my back—"

It was useless to reason with him. Culver let him go on until he had exhausted his bitter spurt of hatred, of poison, and until finally he lay back again with a groan in the weeds—only a moment before the cry came again: "Saddle up! Saddle up!"

They pushed off once more. It was just a bit easier now, for they were to walk for two miles on the highway, where there was no sand to hinder their steps, before turning back onto the side roads. Yet there was a comfortless feeling at the outset, too: legs cramped and aching from the moment's rest, he walked stooped and bent over, at the start, like an arthritic old man, and he was sweating again, dry with thirst, after only a hundred yards. How on earth, he wondered, gazing up for a second at the dim placid landscape of stars, would they last until the next morning, until nearly noon? A car passed them—a slick convertible bound for the North, New York perhaps—wherever, inevitably, for some civilian pleasure—and its fleet, almost soundless passage brought, along with the red pinpoint of its vanishing taillights, a new sensation of unreality to the night, the march: dozing, shrouded by the dark, its people seemed unaware of the shadowy walkers, had sped unceasingly on, like ocean voyagers oblivious of all those fishy struggles below them in the night, submarine and fathomless.

They plodded on, the Colonel pacing the

march, but slower now, and Culver played desperately with the idea that the man would, somehow, tire, become exhausted himself. A wild fantasia of hopes and imaginings swept through his mind: that Templeton *would* become fatigued, having overestimated his own strength, *would* stop the march after an hour or so and load them on the trucks—like a stern father who begins a beating, only to become touched with if not remorse then leniency, and stays his hand. But Culver knew it was a hollow desire. They pushed relentlessly ahead, past shadowy pine groves, fields dense with the fragrance of alfalfa and wild strawberries, shuttered farmhouses, deserted rickety stores. Then this brief civilized vista they abandoned again, and for good, when without pause they plunged off again onto another road, into the sand. Culver had become bathed in sweat once more; they all had, even the Colonel, whose neat dungarees had a black triangular wet spot plastered at their back. Culver heard his own breath coming hoarsely again, and felt the old panic: he'd never be able to make it, he knew, he'd fall out on the side like the old man he was—

but far back to the rear then he heard Mannix's huge voice, dominating the night: "All
right, goddammit, move out! We got sand here
now. Move out and close it up! Close it up,
I say, goddammit! Leadbetter, get that barn
out of your ass and close it up! *Close it up,*
I say!" They spurred Culver on, after a fashion, but following upon those shouts, there
was a faint, subdued chorus, almost inaudi-
ble, of moans and protests. They came only
from Mannix's company, a muffled, sullen
groan. To them Culver heard his own fitful
breath add a groan—expressing something he
could hardly put a name to: fury, despair,
approaching doom—he scarcely knew. He
stumbled on behind the Colonel, like a ewe
who follows the slaughterhouse ram, dumb
and undoubting, too panicked by the general
chaos to hate its leader, or care.

At the end of the second hour, and three
more miles, Culver was sobbing with exhaustion. He flopped down in the weeds, conscious
now of a blister beginning at the bottom of
his foot, as if it had been scraped by a razor.

Mannix was having trouble, too. This
time when he came up, he was limping. He

sat down silently and took off his shoe; Culver, gulping avidly at his canteen, watched him. Both of them were too winded to smoke, or to speak. They were sprawled beside some waterway—canal or stream; phosphorescent globes made a spooky glow among shaggy Spanish moss, and a rank and fetid odor bloomed in the darkness—not the swamp's decay, Culver realized, but Mannix's feet. "Look," the Captain muttered suddenly, "that nail's caught me right in the heel." Culver peered down by the glare of Mannix's flashlight to see on his heel a tiny hole, bleeding slightly, bruised about its perimeter and surrounded by a pasty white where the band-aid had been pulled away. "How'm I going to do it with that?" Mannix said.

"Try beating that nail down again."

"I tried, but the point keeps coming out. I'd have to take the whole frigging shoe apart."

"Can't you put a piece of cloth over it or something?"

"I tried that, too, but it puts my foot off balance. It's worse than the nail." He paused. "Jesus Christ."

"Look," Culver said, "try taking this strip of belt and putting it over it." They debated, operated, talked hurriedly, and neither of them was aware of the Colonel, who had walked over through the shadows and was standing beside them. "What's the matter, Captain?" he said.

They looked up, startled. Hands hooked as usual—Culver wanted to say "characteristically"—in his belt, he stood serenely above them. In the yellow flashlight glow his face was red from exertion, still damp with sweat, but he appeared no more fatigued than a man who had sprinted a few yards to catch a bus. The faint smile hovered at the corners of his lips. Once more it was neither complacent nor superior but, if anything, almost benevolent, so that by the unnatural light, in which his delicate features became fiery red and again now, along the borders of his slim tapering fingers, nearly transparent, he looked still not so much the soldier but the priest in whom passion and faith had made an alloy, at last, of only the purest good intentions; above meanness or petty spite, he was leading a march to some humorless salvation, and his smile—his solicitous words, too —had at least a bleak sincerity.

"I got a nail in my shoe," Mannix said.

The Colonel squatted down and inspected Mannix's foot, cupping it almost tenderly in his hand. Mannix appeared to squirm at the Colonel's touch. "That looks bad," he said after a moment, "did you see the corpsman?"

"No, sir," Mannix replied tensely, "I don't think there's anything can be done. Unless I had a new pair of boondockers."

The Colonel ruminated, rubbing his chin, his other hand still holding the Captain's foot. His eyes searched the dark reaches of the surrounding swamp, where now the rising moon had laid a tranquil silver dust. Frogs piped shrilly in the night, among the cypress and the shallows and closer now, by the road and the stagnant canal, along which danced shifting pinpoints of fire—cigarettes that rose and fell in the hidden fingers of exhausted men. "Well," the Colonel finally said, "well—" and paused. Again the act: indecision before decision, the waiting. "Well," he said, and paused again. The waiting. At that moment—in a wave that came up through his thirst, his throbbing lips, his numb sense of futility—Culver felt that he knew of no one on earth he had ever loathed so much before. And his fury was heightened by the knowledge that he did not hate the man—the Templeton with his shrewd friendly eyes and harmless swagger, that fatuous man whose attempt to convey some impression of a deep and subtle wisdom was almost endearing—not this man, but the Colonel, the marine: that was the one he despised. He didn't hate him for himself, nor even for his brutal march. Bad as it was, there were no doubt worse ordeals; it was at least a peaceful landscape they had to cross. But he did hate him for his perverse and brainless gesture: squatting in the sand, gently, almost indecently now, stroking Mannix's foot, he had too long been conditioned by the system to perform with grace a human act. Too ignorant to know that with this gesture—so nakedly human in the midst of a crazy, capricious punishment which he himself had imposed—he lacerated the Captain by his very touch. Then he spoke. Culver knew what he was going to say. Nothing could have been worse.

"Well," he said, "maybe you'd better ride in on one of the trucks."

If there had been ever the faintest possibility that Mannix would ride in, those words shattered it. Mannix drew his foot away abruptly, as if the Colonel's hand were acid, or fire. "No, sir!" he said fiercely—too fiercely, the note of antagonism, now, was unmistakable— "No, sir! I'll make this frigging march." Furiously, he began to put on his shoe. The Colonel rose to his feet, hooked his thumbs in his belt and gazed carelessly down.

"I think you're going to regret it," he said, "with that foot of yours."

The Captain got up, limping off toward his company, over his retreating shoulder shot back a short, clipped burst of words at the Colonel—whose eyeballs rolled white with astonishment when he heard them— and thereby joined the battle.

"Who cares what you think," he said.

IV

Had the Colonel entertained any immediate notions of retribution, he held them off, for at a quarter past four that morning—halfway through the march, when the first green light of dawn streaked the sky—Culver still heard Mannix's hoarse, ill-tempered voice, lashing his troops from the rear. For hours he had lost track of Mannix. As for the Colonel, the word had spread that he was no longer pacing the march but had gone somewhere to the rear and was walking there. In his misery, a wave of hope swelled up in Culver: if the Colonel had become fagged, and was walking no longer but sitting in his jeep somewhere, at least they'd all have the consolation of having succeeded while their leader failed. But it was a hope, Culver knew, that was ill-founded. He'd be back there slogging away. The bastard could outmarch twenty men, twenty raging Mannixes.

The hike had become disorganized, no slower but simply more spread out. Culver—held back by fatigue and thirst and the

burning, enlarging pain in his feet—found
himself straggling behind. From time to
time he managed to catch up; at one point
he discovered himself at the tail end of Mannix's company, but he no longer really cared.
The night had simply become a great solitude
of pain and thirst, and an exhaustion so profound that it enveloped his whole spirit,
and precluded thought.

A truck rumbled past, loaded with supine
marines, so still they appeared unconscious.
Another passed, and another—they came all
night. But far to the front, long after each
truck's passage, he could hear Mannix's cry:
"Keep on, Jack! This company's walking in."
They pushed on through the night, a sham-
bling horde of zombies in drenched dungarees, eyes transfixed on the earth in a sort of
glazed, avid concentration. After midnight it
seemed to Culver that his mind only regis-
tered impressions, and these impressions had
no sequence but were projected upon his brain
in a scattered, disordered riot, like a movie
film pieced together by an idiot. His memory went back no further than the day before; he no longer thought of anything so un-

attainable as home. Even the end of the march seemed a fanciful thing, beyond all possibility, and what small aspirations he now had were only to endure this one hour, if just to attain the microscopic bliss of ten minutes' rest and a mouthful of warm water. And bordering his memory was ever the violent and haunting picture of the mangled bodies he had seen—when? where? it seemed weeks, years ago, beneath the light of an almost prehistoric sun; try as he could, to dwell upon consoling scenes—home, music, sleep—his mind was balked beyond that vision: the shattered youth with slumbering eyes, the blood, the swarming noon.

Then at the next halt, their sixth—or seventh, eighth, Culver had long ago lost count —he saw Mannix lying beside a jeep-towed water-cart at the rear of his company. O'Leary was sprawled out next to him, breath coming in long asthmatic groans. Culver eased himself painfully down beside them and touched Mannix's arm. The light of dawn, a feverish pale green, had begun to appear, outlining on Mannix's face a twisted look of suffering. His eyes were closed.

"How you doing, Al?" Culver said, reaching up to refill his canteen.

"Hotsy-totsy," he breathed, "except for my frigging foot. How you making it, boy?" His voice was listless. Culver looked down at Mannix's shoe; he had taken it off, to expose heel and sock, where, soaked up like the wick of a lantern, rose a dark streak of blood.

"Jesus," Culver said, "Al, for Christ sake now, you'd better ride in on a truck."

"Nail's out, sport. I finally stole me a pair of pliers, some radioman. Had to run like hell to catch up."

"Even so—" Culver began. But Mannix had fallen into an impervious silence. Up the road stretched a line of squatting men, Mannix's company. Most were sprawled in the weeds or the dust of the road in attitudes as stiff as death, yet some nearby sat slumped over their rifles, drinking water, smoking; there was a thin resentful muttering in the air. And the men close at hand—the faces he could see in the indecisive light—wore looks of agonized and silent protest. They seemed to be mutely seeking for the Captain,

author of their misery, and they were like
faces of men in bondage who had jettisoned
all hope, and were close to defeat. In the
weeds Mannix breathed heavily, mingling
his with the tortured wheezes of O'Leary,
who had fallen sound asleep. It was getting
hot again. No one spoke. Then a fitful rum-
bling filled the dawn, grew louder, and along
the line bodies stirred, heads turned, gazing
eastward down the road at an oncoming,
roaring cloud of dust. Out of the dust came
a machine. It was a truck, and it passed them,
and it rattled to a stop up in the midst of the
company.

"Anyone crapped out here?" a voice
called. "I got room for ten more."

There was a movement toward the truck;
nearby, half a dozen men got to their feet,
slung their rifles, and began to hobble up the
road. Culver watched them tensely, hearing
Mannix stir beside him, putting his shoe
back on. O'Leary had awakened and sat up.
Together the three of them watched the procession toward the truck: a straggle of limping men plodding as wretchedly as dog-
pound animals toward that yawning vehicle

in the smoky dawn, huge, green, and possessed of wheels—which would deliver them
to freedom, to sleep, oblivion. Mannix
watched them without expression, through inflamed eyes; he seemed so drugged, so
dumb with exhaustion, that he was unaware
of what was taking place. "What happened to
the Colonel?" he said absently.

"He went off in a jeep a couple of hours
ago," O'Leary said, "said something about
checking on the column of march."

"What?" Mannix said. Again, he seemed
unaware of the words, as if they—like the
sight of this slow streaming exodus toward
the truck—were making no sudden imprint
on his mind, but were filtering into his con-
sciousness through piles and layers of wool.
A dozen more men arose and began a lame
procession toward the truck. Mannix watched
them, blinking. "What?" he repeated.

"To check the column, sir," O'Leary repeated. "That's what he said."

"He *did?*" Mannix turned with an angry,
questioning look. "Who's pacing the march,
then?"

"Major Lawrence is."

"He *is?*" Mannix rose to his feet, precariously, stiffly and in pain balancing himself not on the heel, but the toe only, of his wounded foot. He blinked in the dawn, gazing at the rear of the truck and the cluster of marines there, feebly lifting themselves into the interior. He said nothing and Culver, watching him from below, could only think of the baffled fury of some great bear cornered, bloody and torn by a foe whose tactics were no braver than his own, but simply more cunning. He bit his lips—out of pain perhaps, but as likely out of impotent rage and frustration, and he seemed close to tears when he said, in a tone almost like grief: "*He* crapped out! *He* crapped out!"

He came alive like a somnambulist abruptly shocked out of sleep, and he lunged forward onto the road with a wild and tormented bellow. "Hey, you people, get off that goddam truck!" He sprang into the dust with a skip and a jump, toiling down the road with hobbled leg and furious flailing arms. By his deep swinging gait, his terrible limp, he looked no more capable of locomotion than a wheel-chair invalid, and it would

have been funny had it not seemed at the
same time so full of threat and disaster. He
pressed on. "Off that truck, goddammit, I say!
Off that truck. Saddle up. Saddle up now, I
say! On your feet!" he yelled. "Get off that
goddam truck before I start kicking you people in the ass!" His words flayed and cowed
them; a long concerted groan arose in the
air, seemed to take possession of the very
dawn; yet they debarked from the truck in
terrified flight, scuttling down like mice
from a sinking raft. "Move the hell out of
here!" he shouted at the truck driver, a
skinny corporal, eyes bulging, who popped
back into the cab in fright. "Get that heap
out of here!" The truck leaped off with a
roar, enveloping the scene in blue smoke and
a tornado of dust. Mannix, with windmilling
arms, stood propped on his toe in the center
of the road, urged the men wildly on. "Saddle up now! Let somebody else crap out O.K.,
but not you people, hear me! Do you hear
me! Goddammit, I mean it! Shea, get those
people moving out up there! You people better face it, you got eighteen more miles to

go . . ." Culver tried to stop him, but they had already begun to run.

Panic-stricken, limping with blisters and with exhaustion, and in mutinous despair, the men fled westward, whipped on by Mannix's cries. They pressed into the humid, sweltering light of the new day. Culver followed; O'Leary, without a murmur, puffed along beside him, while to the rear, with steady slogging footsteps, trailed the remnants of the battalion. Dust billowed up and preceded them, like Egypt's pillar of cloud, filling the air with its dry oppressive menace. It coated their lips and moist brows with white powdery grit, like a spray of plaster, and gave to the surrounding trees, the underbrush and vacant fields, a blighted pallor, as if touched by unseasonable frost. The sun rose higher, burning down at their backs so that each felt he bore on his shoulders not the burden of a pack but, almost worse, a portable oven growing hotter and hotter as the sun came up from behind the sheltering pines. They walked automatically, no longer with that light and tentative step in order to ease the pain in their feet, but with the firm, dogged tread of robots; and if they were all like Culver they had long since parted with a sensation of motion below the hips, and felt there only a constant throbbing pain—of blisters and battered muscles and the protest of exhausted bones.

Then one time Culver saw the Colonel go by in a jeep, boiling along in a cloud of dust toward the head of the column. He caught a glimpse of him as he passed: he looked sweaty and tired, far from rested, and Culver wondered how justified Mannix's outrage had been, assigning to the Colonel that act of cowardice. So he hadn't been pacing the march, but God knows he must have been hiking along to the rear; and his doubts were bolstered by O'Leary's voice, coming painfully beside him: "Old Captain Mannix's mighty pissed off at the Colonel." He paused, wheezing steadily. "Don't know if he's got a right to be that way. Old Colonel ain't gonna crap out without a reason. Colonel's kind of rough sometimes but he'll go with the troops." Culver said nothing. They plodded ahead silently. Culver felt like cursing the Sergeant.

How could he be so stupid? How could he, in the midst of this pain, yield up still only words of accord and respect and even admiration for the creator of such a wild and lunatic punishment? Only a man so firmly cemented to the system that all doubts were beyond countenance could say what O'Leary did—and yet—and yet God knows, Culver thought wearily, he could be right and himself and Mannix, and the rest of them, inescapably wrong. His mind was confused. A swarm of dust came up and filled his lungs. Mannix was screwing everything up horribly, and Culver wanted suddenly to sprint forward—in spite of the effort it took—reach the Captain, take him aside and tell him: *Al, Al, let up, you've already lost the battle.* Defiance, pride, endurance—none of these would help. He only mutilated himself by this perverse and violent rebellion; no matter what the Colonel was—coward and despot or staunch bold leader—he had him beaten, going and coming. Nothing could be worse than what Mannix was doing—adding to a disaster already ordained (Culver somehow sensed) the burden of his vicious fury. At least let up, the men had had enough. But his mind was confused. His kidneys were aching as if they had been pounded with a mallet, and he walked along now with his hands on his waist, like a professor lecturing in a classroom, coattails over his arms.

And for the first time he felt intolerably hot—with a heat that contributed to his mounting fury. At night they had sweated more from exertion; the coolness of the evening had been at least some solace, but the morning's sun began to flagellate him anew, adding curious sharp blades of pain to the furious frustration boiling inside him. Frustration at the fact that he was not independent enough, nor possessed of enough free will, was not *man* enough to say, to hell with it and crap out himself; that he was not man enough to disavow all his determination and endurance and suffering, cash in his chips, and by that act flaunt his contempt of the march, the Colonel, the whole bloody Marine Corps. But he was *not* man enough, he knew, far less simply a free man; he was just a marine—as was Mannix, and so many of the others—and they had been marines, it seemed, all their lives, would go on being marines forever; and the frustration implicit in this thought brought him suddenly close to tears. Mannix. A cold horror came over him. Far down, profoundly, Mannix was so much a marine that it could make him casually demented. The corruption begun years ago in his drill-field feet had climbed up, overtaken him, and had begun to rot his brain. Culver heard himself sobbing with frustration and outrage. The sun beat down against his back. His mind slipped off into fevered blankness, registering once more, on that crazy cinematic tape, chaos, vagrant jigsaw images: Mannix's voice far ahead, hoarse and breaking now, then long spells of silence; halts beside stifling, windless fields, then a shady ditch into which he plunged, feverish and comatose, dreaming of a carnival tent where one bought, from a dozen barrels, all sorts of ice, chipped, crushed, and cubed, in various shapes and sizes. He was awakened by that terrible cry—*Saddle up, saddle up!*—and he set out again. The sun rose higher and higher. O'Leary, with a groan, dropped behind and vanished. Two trucks passed loaded with stiff, green-clad bodies motionless as corpses. The canteen fell off Culver's belt, somewhere, sometime; now he found though, to his surprise, that he was no longer thirsty and no longer sweating. This was dangerous, he recalled from some lecture, but at that moment the young marine vomiting at the roadside seemed more important, even more interesting. He stopped to help, thought better of it, passed on—through a strange crowd of pale and tiny butterflies, borne like bleached petals in shimmering slow-motion across the dusty road. At one point Hobbs, the radioman, cruised by in a jeep with a fishpole antenna; he was laughing, taunting the marchers with a song—*I got romance in my pants*—and he waved a jolly fat hand. A tanager rose, scarlet and beautiful, from a steaming thicket and pinwheeled upward, down again, and into the meadow beyond: there Culver thought, for a brief terrified moment, that he saw eight butchered corpses lying in a row, blood streaming out against the weeds. But it passed. Of course, he remembered, that was yesterday—or was it?—and then for minutes he tried to recall

Hobbs's name, gave up the effort; it was along about this time, too, that he gazed at his watch, neither pleased nor saddened to find that it was not quite nine o'clock, began to wind it with careful absorption as he trudged along, and looked up to see Mannix looming enormously at the roadside.

"Get up," the Captain was saying. He had hardly any voice left at all; whatever he spoke with gave up only a rasp, a whisper. "Get your ass off the deck," he was saying, "get up, I say."

Culver stopped and watched. The marine lay back in the weeds. He was fat and he had a three-day growth of beard. He held up one bare foot, where there was a blister big as a silver dollar and a dead, livid white, the color of a toadstool; as the Captain spoke, the marine blandly peeled the skin away, revealing a huge patch of tender, pink, virgin flesh. He had a patient hillbilly voice and he was explaining softly, "Ah just cain't go on, Captain, with a foot like this. Ah just cain't do it, and that's all there is to it."

"You *can*, goddammit," he rasped. "I

walked ten miles with a nail in my foot. If I can do it you can, too. Get up, I said. You're a marine . . ."

"Captain," he went on patiently, "Ah cain't help it about your nail. Ah may be a marine and all that but Ah ain't no goddam fool . . ."

The Captain, poised on his crippled foot, made a swift, awkward gesture toward the man, as if to drag him to his feet; Culver grabbed him by the arm, shouting furiously: "Stop it, Al! Stop it! Stop it! Stop it! Enough!" He paused, looking into Mannix's dull hot eyes. "Enough!" he said, more quietly. "Enough." Then gently, "That's enough, Al. They've just had enough." The end was at hand, Culver knew, there was no doubt of that. The march had come to a halt again, the men lay sprawled out on the sweltering roadside. He looked at the Captain, who shook his head dumbly and suddenly ran trembling fingers over his eyes. "O.K.," he murmured, "yeah . . . yes"—something incoherent and touched with grief—and Culver felt tears running down his cheeks. He was too tired to think—except: old Al. Mannix. Goddam. "They've had enough," he repeated.

Mannix jerked his hand away from his face. "O.K.," he croaked, "Christ sake, I hear you. O.K. They've had enough, they've had enough. O.K. I heard you the first time. Let 'em crap out! I've did—done—" He paused, wheeled around. "To hell with them all."

He watched Mannix limp away. The Colonel was standing nearby up the road, thumbs hooked in his belt, regarding the Captain soberly. Culver's spirit sank like a rock. Old Al, he thought. You just couldn't win. Goddam. Old great soft scarred bear of a man.

If in defeat he appeared despondent, he retained one violent shred of life which sustained him to the end—his fury. It would get him through. He was like a man running a gauntlet of whips, who shouts outrage and defiance at his tormentors until he falls at the finish. Yet—as Culver could have long ago foretold—it was a fury that was uncontained; the old smoking bonfire had blazed up in his spirit. And if it had been out of control hours ago when he had first defied the Colonel, there was no doubt at all that now it could not fail to consume both of them. At least one of them. Culver, prone on his belly in the weeds, was hot with tension, and he felt blood pounding at his head when he heard the Colonel call, in a frosty voice: "Captain Mannix, will you come here a minute?"

Culver was the closest at hand. There were six more miles to go. The break had extended this time to fifteen minutes—an added rest because, as Culver had heard the Colonel explain to the Major, they'd walk the last six miles without a halt. Another break, he'd said, with a wry weary grin, and they'd never be able to get the troops off the ground. Culver had groaned—another senseless piece of sadism—then reasoned wearily that it *was* a good idea. Probably. Maybe. Who knew? He was too tired to care. He watched Mannix walk with an awful hobbling motion up the road, face screwed up in pain and eyes asquint like a man trying to gaze at the sun. He moved at a good rate of speed but his gait was terrible to behold—jerks and spasms which warded off, reacted to, or vainly tried to control great zones and areas of pain. Behind him most of his men lay in stupefied rows at the edge of the road and waited for the trucks to come. They knew Mannix had finished, and they had crumpled completely. For the last ten minutes, in a listless fashion, he had assembled less than a third of the company who were willing to continue the march —diehards, athletes, and just those who, like Mannix himself, would make the last six miles out of pride and spite. Out of fury. It was a seedy, bedraggled column of people: of hollow, staring eyes and faces green with slack-jawed exhaustion; and behind them the remnants of the battalion made hardly more than two hundred men. Mannix struggled on up the road, approached the Colonel, and stood there propped on his toe, hands on his hips for balance.

The Colonel looked at him steadily for a moment, coldly. Mannix was no longer a simple doubter but the heretic, and was about to receive judgment. Yet there was still an almost paternal reluctance in Templeton's voice as he spoke, slowly and very softly, out of the troops' hearing: "Captain Mannix, I want you to go in on the trucks."

"No, sir," Mannix said hoarsely, "I'm going to make this march."

The Colonel looked utterly whipped; gray bags of fatigue hung beneath his eyes. He seemed no longer to have strength enough to display his odd theatrical smile; his posture was taut and vaguely stooped, the unmistakable bent-kneed stance of a man with blisters, and Culver was forced to concede—with a sense of mountainous despair—that he *had* made the march after all, somewhere toward the rear and for legitimate reasons of his own, even if Mannix now was too blind, too outraged, to tell. *Goddam*, Culver heard himself moaning aloud, *if just he only hadn't made it*, but he heard the Colonel go on coolly: "Not with that foot you aren't." He glanced down. The Captain's ankle had swollen to a fat milky purple above the top of his shoe; he was unable to touch his heel to the ground even if he had wanted to. "Not with that foot," he repeated.

Mannix was silent, panting deeply—not as

if taken aback at all, but only as if gathering
wind for an outburst. He and the Colonel
gazed at each other, twin profiles embattled
against an escarpment of pines, the chaste
blue sky of morning. "Listen, Colonel," he
rasped, "you ordered this goddam hike and
I'm going to walk it even if I haven't got one
goddam man left. You can crap out yourself
for half the march—" Culver wanted desperately, somehow, by any means to stop him—
not just because he was pulling catastrophe
down on his head but because it was simply
no longer worth the effort. Couldn't he see?
That the Colonel didn't care and that was
that? That with him the hike had had nothing
to do with courage or sacrifice or suffering,
but was only a task to be performed, that
whatever he was he was no coward, he had
marched the whole way—or most of it, any
idiot could see that—and that he was as far
removed from the vulgar battle, the competi-
tion, which Mannix had tried to promote as
the frozen, remotest stars. He just didn't care.
Culver strove, in a sick, heaving effort, to
rise, to go and somehow separate them, but

Mannix was charging on: "You run your troops. Fine. O.K. But what's all this about crapping out—"

"Wait a minute, Captain, now—" the Colonel blurted ominously. "For your information—"

"*Fuck* you and your information," said Mannix in a hoarse, choked voice. He was almost sobbing. "If you think—"

But he went no further, for the Colonel had made a curious, quick gesture—stage-gesture, fantastic and subtle, and it was like watching an old cowboy film to see the Colonel's hand go swiftly back to the handle of his pistol and rest there, his eyes cool and passionate and forbidding. It was a gesture of force which balked even the Captain. Mannix's face went pale—as if he had only just then realized the words which had erupted so heedlessly from his mouth—and he said nothing, only stood there sullen and beaten and blinking at the glossy white handle of the pistol as the Colonel went on: "For your information, Captain, you aren't the only one who made this march. But I'm not *interested* in your observations. You quiet down now,

hear? You march in, see? I order you confined to your quarters, and I'm going to see
that you get a court-martial. Do you understand? I'm going to have you tried for gross
insubordination. I'll have you sent to Korea.
Keep your mouth shut. Now get back to your
company!" He was shaking with wrath; the
hot morning light beat with piety and with
vengeance from his gray, outraged eyes. "Get
back to your men," he whispered, *"get back
to your men!"*

Then he turned his back to the Captain and
called down the road to the Major: "All
right, Billy, let's saddle up!"

So it was over, but not quite all. The last
six miles took until past noon. Mannix's per-
petual tread on his toe alone gave to his gait
a ponderous, bobbing motion which resem-
bled that of a man wretchedly spastic and
paralyzed. It lent to his face too—whenever
Culver became detached from his own misery
long enough to glance at him—an aspect of
deep, almost prayerfully passionate concentration—eyes thrown skyward and lips fluttering feverishly in pain—so that if one did
not know he was in agony one might imagine

that he was a communicant in rapture, offering up breaths of hot desire to the heavens. It was impossible to imagine such a distorted face; it was the painted, suffering face of a clown, and the heaving gait was a grotesque and indecent parody of a hopeless cripple, with shoulders gyrating like a seesaw and with flapping, stricken arms. The Colonel and the Major had long since outdistanced them, and Culver and Mannix walked alone. When the base came into sight, he was certain they were not going to make it. They trudged into the camp. Along the barren, treeless streets marines in neat khaki were going to lunch, and they turned to watch the mammoth gyrating Captain, so tattered and soiled—who addressed convulsive fluttering prayers to the sky, and had obviously parted with his senses. Then Mannix stopped suddenly and grasped Culver's arm. "What the hell," he whispered, "we've made it."

V

For a long while Culver was unable to sleep. He had lain naked on his bed for what seemed hours, but unconsciousness would not come; his closed eyes offered up only vistas of endless roads, steaming thickets, fields, tents— sunshine and darkness illogically commingled—and the picture, which returned to his mind with the unshakable regularity of a scrap of music, of the boys who lay dead beneath the light of another noon. Try as he could, sleep would not come. So he dragged himself erect and edged toward the window, laboriously, because of his battered feet; it took him a full minute to do so, and his legs, like those of an amputee which possess the ghost of sensation, felt as if they were still in motion, pacing endless distances. He lowered himself into a chair and lighted a cigarette. Below, the swimming pool was grotto-blue, a miniature of the cloudless sky above, lit with shapes of dancing light as shiny as silver dimes. A squad of sunsuited maidens, officers' wives, splashed at its brink or ate ice-cream sundaes on the lawn, and filled the noontime with their decorous sunny laughter. It was hot and still. Far off above the pines, in the hot sunlight and over distant peace and civilization, brewed the smoky and threatful beginnings of a storm.

Culver let his head fall on his arm. Yes, they had had it—those eight boys—he thought, there was no doubt of that. In mindless slumber now, they were past caring, though diadems might drop or Doges surrender. They were ignorant of all. And that they had never grown old enough to know anything, even the tender miracle of pity, was perhaps a better ending—it was hard to tell. Faint warm winds came up from the river, bearing with them a fragrance of swamp and pine, and a last whisper of air passed through the trees, shuddered, died, became still; suddenly Culver felt a deep vast hunger for something he could not explain, nor ever could remember having known quite so achingly before. He only felt that all of his life he had yearned for something that was as fleeting and as incommunicable, in its beauty, as that one bar of music he remembered, or those lovely little girls with their ever joyful, ever sprightly dance on some far and fantastic lawn—serenity, a quality of repose—he could not call it by name, but only knew that, somehow, it had always escaped him. As he sat there, with the hunger growing and blossoming within him, he felt that he had hardly ever known a time in his life when he was not marching or sick with loneliness or afraid.

And so, he thought, they had all had it, in their various fashions. The Colonel had had his march and his victory, and Culver could not say still why he was unable to hate him. Perhaps it was only because he was a different kind of man, different enough that he was hardly a man at all, but just a quantity of attitudes so remote from Culver's world that to hate him would be like hating a cannibal, merely because he gobbled human flesh. At any rate, he had had it. And as for Mannix— well, *he'd* certainly had it, there was no doubt of *that*. Old Al, he thought tenderly. The man with the back unbreakable, the soul of pity— where was he now, great unshatterable vessel of longing, lost in the night, astray at mid-century in the never-endingness of war?

His hunger faded and died. He raised his head and gazed out the window. Over the pool a figure swan-dived against the sky, in cruci-fied, graceless descent broke the water with a lumpy splash. A cloud passed over the day, darkening the lawn with a moment's somber light. The conversation of the girls became subdued, civilized, general. Far off above the trees, on the remotest horizon, thunderheads bloomed, a squall. Later, toward sundown, they would roll landward over a shadowing reach of waves, borne nearer, ever more darkly across the coast, the green wild deso-lation of palmetto and cypress and pine—and here, where the girls pink and scanty in sun-suits would slant their tar-black eyes sky-ward in the gathering night, abandon pool and games and chatter and with shrill cries of warning flee homeward like gaudy scraps of paper on the blast, voices young and lovely and lost in the darkness, the onrushing winds. One thing, Culver thought, was certain—they were in for a blow. Already there would be signals up and down the coast.

Abruptly he was conscious of a dry,

parched thirst. He rose to his feet, put on a
robe, and hobbled out into the hallway toward the water cooler. As he rounded the
corner he saw Mannix, naked except for a
towel around his waist, making his slow and
agonized way down the hall. He was hairy
and enormous and as he inched his way toward the shower room, clawing at the wall
for support, his face with its clenched eyes
and taut, drawn-down mouth was one of tortured and gigantic suffering. The swelling at
his ankle was the size of a grapefruit, an ugly
blue, and this leg he dragged behind him, a
dead weight no longer capable of motion.

Culver started to limp toward him, said,
"Al—" in an effort to help him along, but
just then one of the Negro maids employed
in the place came swinging along with a mop,
stopped, seeing Mannix, ceased the singsong
little tune she was humming, too, and said,
"Oh my, you poor man. What you been doin'?
Do it hurt?" Culver halted.

"Do it hurt?" she repeated. "Oh, I bet it
does. Deed it does." Mannix looked up at her
across the short yards that separated them,
silent, blinking. Culver would remember this:

the two of them communicating across that chasm one unspoken moment of sympathy and understanding before the woman, spectacled, bandannaed, said again, "Deed it does," and before, almost at precisely the same instant, the towel slipped away slowly from Mannix's waist and fell with a soft plop to the floor; Mannix then, standing there, weaving dizzily and clutching for support at the wall, a mass of scars and naked as the day he emerged from his mother's womb, save for the soap which he held feebly in one hand. He seemed to have neither the strength nor the ability to lean down and retrieve the towel and so he merely stood there huge and naked in the slanting dusty light and blinked and sent toward the woman, finally, a sour, apologetic smile, his words uttered, it seemed to Culver, not with self-pity but only with the tone of a man who, having endured and lasted, was too weary to tell her anything but what was true.

"Deed it does," he said.

In the Clap Shack

To Robert D. Loomis

IN THE CLAP SHACK *was first presented on December 15, 1972, at the Yale Repertory Theatre in New Haven, Connecticut, with the following cast:*

WALLACE MAGRUDER, *a hospital patient*	Miles Chapin
SCHWARTZ, *a patient*	Eugene Troobnick
DR. GLANZ, *a urologist*	Jeremy Geidt
LINEWEAVER, *pharmacist's mate first-class*	Nicholas Hormann
CAPTAIN BUDWINKLE, *hospital commandant*	Paul Schierhorn
LORENZO CLARK, *a patient*	Hannibal Penney, Jr.
STANCIK, *a patient*	Joseph G. Grifasi
DADARIO, *a patient*	Michael Gross
MCDANIEL, *a patient*	William Ludel
CHALKLEY, *a patient*	Steven Robman
CATHOLIC CHAPLAIN	Bill Gearhart
CHAPLAIN'S ASSISTANT	Thomas E. Lanter
MARINE CORPORAL, *a military policeman*	Steven Robman

The entire action takes place on the Urological Ward of the United States Naval Hospital at a large Marine Corps base in the South. The time is the summer of 1943.

Act One

The time is the summer of 1943. The place is the Urological Ward of the United States Naval Hospital at a large Marine Corps base in the South. The entire action of the play takes place on this ward, which differs little in appearance from hospital wards throughout the world. Two rows of about nine beds each, their feet facing each other upon a central aisle, dominate the scene. The beds are staggered, so that the audience obtains a view of each bed and its patient. At extreme stage left is the office of the Chief Urologist, DR. GLANZ, *who rules the ward from this cluttered room filled with urological instruments and medical books. To the right of this office, outside the door and at the end of the ward proper, are the chair and desk occupied by Pharmacist's Mate First-Class* LINEWEAVER, GLANZ *'s satrap and the chief male nurse of the ward.*

Overture: "There's a Star-Spangled Banner Waving Somewhere."

As the lights go up on the curtainless stage, it is a few moments before 6:30 A.M., the hour for reveille, and the occupants of the ward are still asleep. Some stir restlessly in their beds. Others snore. One voice is heard to mumble at intervals a small anguished "Pearl! Pearl!" as if in semidelirium. At his desk, LINEWEAVER, *an effeminate, thin, angular sailor in summer whites, sits making out reports with a pencil. Suddenly he looks at his watch and rises, walking slowly down the aisle as he rouses the men. His air is casual, jaunty; the effeminacy should be quite evident but not over-emphasized or caricatured.*

LINEWEAVER *(His voice an amiable singsong)* All right, up and at 'em! Rise and shine, you gyrenes! Drop your cocks and grab your socks! VD patients: short-arm inspection in *precisely ten minutes!*

> *(There are groans from the patients as they rouse themselves. Some sit on the edge of their beds and drowsily regard their feet. Others only prop themselves up against their pillows. One or two manage to stand and stretch, clad like the others in green Marine Corps issue underwear. Only a drowsing Negro—obviously quite sick—and the marine who was heard to mutter "Pearl! Pearl!" remain virtually motionless under their sheets, oblivious to* LINEWEAVER*'s verbal assault. One marine, however,* CORPORAL STANCIK, *rolls over as if to remain resolutely asleep and mumbles his resentment to* LINEWEAVER)*

STANCIK *(His accent is urban, working-class Northeast)* Up yours, Lineweaver, you creep.

LINEWEAVER *(Good-humoredly)* On your feet, Stancik. Dr. Glanz is going to take a look at your tool.

STANCIK   Just let me sleep, you faggot.

LINEWEAVER *(Raps the bed with his hand)* I'm not bullshittin' you this morning, Stancik. Dr. Glanz is going to have the Old Man with him. Captain Budwinkle. And you guys have got to look *very* superior.

> *(*STANCIK *stirs awake as* DADARIO, *a patient standing nearby flexing his muscles and yawning, responds with drowsy sarcasm)*

DADARIO   How can a dozen guys look superior at six-thirty in the morning all lined up with their peckers hanging out?

LINEWEAVER *(Keeping his good humor)* Just use a little imagination, Dadario. *(In a semi-aside)* I think you *all* look *cute.*

STANCIK *(Now climbing out of bed)* You would. *(Yawns)* Boy, did I have a dirty dream.

LINEWEAVER Like I say, Stancik, I think you've got an obsession. It's dreams like that that get you into this joint in the first place.
> *(He pauses at the bedside of the patient who had been calling "Pearl! Pearl!" This is a marine private in his mid-twenties named CHALKLEY. The sick man is now awake but is flushed and sweating, and he has the glassy, distracted look of one who is very ill and in extreme discomfort. LINE-WEAVER takes his pulse and sticks a thermometer in his mouth, then marks something on the chart which is attached to the end of each bed. As he does this, the other patients are frittering the minutes away in various fashions: some leaf through magazines and comic books, a few do desultory setting-up exercises, others resume a three-handed card game, one turns on a portable radio which plays "Don't Fence Me In." Two patients near CHALKLEY's bed, in the meantime, are talking about him)*

DADARIO Did you hear Chalkley? Did you hear him, Schwartz? All night long he kept saying "Pearl, Pearl!" It gave me the creeps. I couldn't sleep. Who do you guess that fucking Pearl is?

SCHWARTZ *(A solemn, bespectacled Jew, perhaps a few years older than the other patients, most of whom are in their early twenties. He raises his eyes from a book)* It's his sister. She's the closest relative he's got. She was run down by a car—in Atlanta, I think. She's in very bad shape. Chalkley told me about her last week, before he got so sick. Poor guy.

DADARIO They should put a guy like that off somewhere by himself, in some room, for his own good and ours. I can't stand to hear him say "Pearl, Pearl!" all night. It gives you the creeps.

SCHWARTZ *(Returns to the book)*   Poor guy.

STANCIK *(To* DADARIO*)*   Are you an ass man or a tit man, Dadario? Me, I'm an ass man. Someday I'm goin' to find me an ass with a pair of handles. Then I'm goin' to really operate.

DADARIO *(He is shaving himself with an electric shaver)* Frankly, I'm for ass *and* tits, Stancik. A sense of proportion is what's needed in the world, if you ask me.

LINEWEAVER *(Pauses at the bed of the Negro, a Southern-born private named* LORENZO CLARK. *The Negro is awake but appears to be very feeble)*   How do you feel this morning, Lorenzo? All bright-eyed and bushy-tailed?

CLARK   Man, I've had better mornin's. Each mornin' 'pears to be a little darker than the last. *(He is speaking very slowly)* How do it feel today?

LINEWEAVER *(Taking his pulse)*   Checks out fine, Lorenzo. Steady as she goes. *(There is a note of false jollity in his voice)* You'll be out of here by Labor Day, eatin' barbecued spareribs and humpin' those little jungle bunnies over in Port Royal like a real stud. Feel like you can down a little chow this morning?

CLARK *(Haltingly)*   I feels pretty poorly. Guess you'd better let me just rest a bit.

LINEWEAVER   Where you headin', gyrene?
(He intercepts a very young marine who is trying politely to press past him. This is a private named WALLY MA-GRUDER. *He is dressed in the same kind of white hospital robe that some of the other patients have already donned. One is struck almost immediately by this boy's bewilder-*

*ment, his vulnerability, and by his wistfulness and inno-
cence)*

MAGRUDER   I—I have to go to the bathroom. I mean, the
head.

LINEWEAVER *(Emphatically)*   Unh-unh! Not till I check your
diagnosis. You're a new face. Didn't you come in last
night during the other duty watch?

MAGRUDER   Yeah, I came in about ten o'clock. I—

LINEWEAVER *(Inspecting* MAGRUDER*'s chart)*   Ah, "Wallace
Magruder, private, serial number five-four-two-three-oh-
seven, age eighteen, born Danville, Virginia. Expert rifle-
man, graduate 417th recruit platoon. Serological tests reveal syphilis." *Syphilis! (Turns to* MAGRUDER *almost
admiringly)* As I live and breathe, a real live syphilitic!
And a three plus on your Kahn *and* your Wassermann—
almost at the top. Aren't *you* the raunchy devil! An aristo-
crat among the votaries of Venus, heir to the malady of
Casanova, De Maupassant and Baudelaire. Welcome
aboard, Magruder. We haven't had a syphilitic in here
since last month. *(Gestures toward the rest of the patients, a
few of whose attention has been caught by the encounter)* Amid
all of this common, garden-variety gonorrhea your afflic-
tion stands out like poison oak. *(An aside)* I'm joking like
crazy, but I'm crying inside. It's *really* almost incurable.

DADARIO *(To* STANCIK*)*   Now *there* is an ass *and* tit man. See
what I mean?

LINEWEAVER   Among these plain old clapped-up types you
walk as a prince among commoners. But you still can't go
to the head.

MAGRUDER *(With pain in his voice)*   Why can't I go to the
head? It's really—

LINEWEAVER   Short-arm inspection, Wally. Every morning, *sharp* at six-forty, a short-arm inspection by Dr. Glanz. And this morning there'll also be Captain Budwinkle, the new hospital commandant.

MAGRUDER   But I've always thought that a short-arm inspection was just for the clap. I mean—
  (*At this moment, a light goes up in the office of the Chief Urologist. Seen entering the room are* DR. GLANZ, *in the uniform of a lieutenant commander, and* CAPTAIN BUD-WINKLE. DR. GLANZ *is a short, officious-looking man with graying hair and spectacles. His every gesture bespeaks obedience to duty and authority.* CAPTAIN BUDWINKLE *looks like a Hollywood version of a Navy captain—imperious, patrician of carriage, aloof and proud. He is decorated with medals and campaign ribbons that go almost to his shoulder.* DR. GLANZ *picks up a sheaf of papers and they converse in pantomine as* LINEWEAVER *continues*)

LINEWEAVER   Pay attention, dopey. It is true that the amount of the clear mucous substance—known amusingly as gleet—which accumulates at the end of the male organ is an index of the effect of treatment for gonorrhea, not syphilis. But since prodigies like yourself are apt in the course of their exploits to pick up *both* diseases, the short-arm is required for you too—at least for the first few days here. Why you are not permitted to pee-pee beforehand should be obvious.

MAGRUDER (*Despairingly*)   All right. God! All right!
  (*As* DR. GLANZ *begins to speak to* CAPTAIN BUDWINKLE, *the patients continue their early morning routine. It should be made plain that the conversation between the two officers is out of the patients' earshot*)

GLANZ   We think it's a sign, Captain Budwinkle, of the moral breakdown this war has brought about that we've seen a truly alarming rise in the incidence of venereal cases. As the Captain well knows, venereal disease has always been with us in the Navy and Marine Corps. It's a major problem. But never before have we, personally, witnessed such a shocking growth.

BUDWINKLE Well, Dr. Glanz, I appreciate your concern about the VD crisis. Of course I'm no doctor, but as an administrator, I'm quite alarmed. Washington is also very much alarmed. Needless to say, I am not here at this ungodly hour for beer and skittles. One of my first and most urgent duties on assuming this command is to get an accurate bearing on our venereal situation. To get a clear view from the poop deck, that is, so we can navigate the rocks and shoals.

GLANZ Well, sir, nothing would be more revealing than a breakdown of the composition of this one urological ward. (*Gestures with his hand at a chart*) Of our fifteen patients only four are here for *non*-venereal reasons. The most serious is a case of pyelonephritis—chronic, we're afraid. Should have been nipped at the first physical exam, but wasn't, so now he'll die at government expense. It's definitely a terminal case, since the patient has developed galloping hypertension. Our second non-VD is a simple circumcision. Our third is a kidney calculus. Our fourth and last is suspected renal tuberculosis. Jewish chap. No worry about circumcision *there*, eh, sir? (*Chuckles*) Well, the rest of our patients are entirely venereal, practically all gonorrhea. It's a thoroughly corrupt and discouraging scene, as the Captain will shortly see.

BUDWINKLE Just how well do your gonorrhea cases seem to be responding to the newer sulfa drugs, Glanz? If they're doing as poorly as I've heard elsewhere we'd better batten down all ports and hatches and man the fire stations.

GLANZ Generally speaking, your information is correct, sir, though we've seen great improvement in a few individual cases.

BUDWINKLE I gather that among your venereal patients you have a case of granuloma inguinale. How does it seem to be responding to sulfa?

GLANZ Not at all, so far as we can tell, Captain. This colored boy has a badly ulcerated groin and is severely debilitated. We frankly don't give him much hope. He may linger for a while, though. We, personally, thank God that granuloma is confined almost exclusively to the Negro race.

BUDWINKLE Also it's an extremely repellent disease, with high mortality.

GLANZ Yes, sir. We sometimes shudder to think what might happen if granuloma were easily contracted by our white marines and sailor boys. God knows they are promiscuous enough as it is.

BUDWINKLE You know, Glanz, I've heard recently of a remarkable new drug, developed in England. I believe it's called penicillin. (*Puts accent on the wrong syllable*) So far it's worked miracles on all sorts of previously intractable infectious diseases. Unfortunately, I gather it won't be available to our Navy until sometime next year.

GLANZ Penicillin, sir. Yes, we've heard about the drug. Could be a godsend. But won't it offer grave problems besides, sir?

BUDWINKLE How's that, Doctor?

GLANZ Well, if it becomes the specific drug of therapy in most venereal cases, won't this open up the floodgates of vice? For if a libertine knows that he can indulge himself with impunity, he will throw all caution to the winds. What universal debauchery this might portend for our nation!

BUDWINKLE God forbid, Dr. Glanz.

GLANZ Meanwhile, sir, we make do, make do. Old-fashioned moral outrage simply does not seem to be sufficient. Also, we suspend the pay and allowances of these VD cases. It should be a deterrent, but it isn't. So in the end it looks as if there is absolutely nothing to prevent them from copulating like rabbits, and without even taking the precaution of using the condoms and the prophylaxis we dispense free. Free, sir! Free!

BUDWINKLE The most powerful—I should say, the most *influential*—forces in Washington would tend to support your view, Glanz. On the other hand, there's a faction of namby-pamby and bleeding-heart liberals in the Navy department and in the government generally who'd like to try to minimize the atrocious nature of venereal disease. They'd propose to eliminate it entirely as an offense on a serviceman's record. *(Makes a mock-effeminate gesture)* Freshwater la-de-das! If you want to know my candid opinion, Glanz, and it's strictly entre nous—this faction has been heavily influenced by the thinking of Eleanor Roosevelt.

LINEWEAVER Fall in for short-arm inspection!
(The VD patients begin to form a rank in front of their respective beds)

BUDWINKLE We've spoken of gonorrhea. What's the situation here vis-à-vis syphilis?

GLANZ Runs a poor second to gonorrhea, sir, but of course we get many cases. Syphilis! That bedraggled old tart still gives us lots of surprises and unless nipped in the bud is virtually incurable. For instance, only last night a lad came in—young marine of eighteen, you'll see him in a moment—with an unbelievable positive Wassermann. I'm convinced his syphilis is far advanced, but diagnosis remains doggone tough, if we might say so, sir. He disclaims having observed any of the other standard symptoms. He also refuses to admit to any promiscuity. We suspect with this particular boy it's a simple case of *lying*. His manner was very devious, we thought, and—well, frankly, he has the soft, full mouth of a voluptuary.

BUDWINKLE *(Chuckles)*   It shouldn't be too hard to find the cut of *his* jib. Quite simply, it would seem to me that if you dip down into this boy's sexual history you might come up with a real bucketful of worms.

GLANZ   Oh, yes, sir, the Captain is dead on target there! That's *most* essential. A detailed examination of a venereal patient's sexual profile is often the key to a successful diagnosis.

LINEWEAVER *(At the office door)*   VD patients all assembled for short-arm, sir. *(Shouts to patients)* Attention on deck!

GLANZ   Thank you, Lineweaver. *(They enter the ward)* Nothing has supplanted the old short-arm to determine the progress of therapy, Captain. It may seem a primitive method of examination in this advanced era, but no one has yet devised a better one.
   (The patients are lined up in front of their beds. Accompanied by LINEWEAVER *and* BUDWINKLE, GLANZ *advances down the line, pausing first in front of* DADARIO*)*

LINEWEAVER *(Stares suggestively at* DADARIO*'s groin)*   Well, bonjour, *big boy*. Skin it back. Squeeze it. Milk it down.

(DADARIO goes through the motion of manipulating his penis, just as the others will)

GLANZ   You're drying up nicely, Dadario. *(To BUDWINKLE)* This is a typical, run-of-the-mine, humdrum case of gonorrhea with no complications, which has responded well to sulfadiazine. Tomorrow there will likely be no urethral discharge, in which case we'll begin to take several smears and cultures for negative gonococci. Then doubtless this lucky lad will be out of here by the end of the week.

BUDWINKLE   I trust you'll walk the straight and narrow from now on out, Dadario. Try to keep that member of yours all buttoned up in your trousers where it belongs. America has a war to wage, but it sure as hell will lose the shooting match if its fighting men persist in waging that war not on the beaches but between the bedsheets. Right, Dadario?

DADARIO   Aye-aye, sir! Thank you, sir. I'll do my best, sir! *(Pauses)* Dr. Glanz, sir, I'd like to register a complaint.

GLANZ   What's that, Dadario?

DADARIO   It's Chalkley there. *(Gestures to the sick man in the next bed)* All night long he keeps hollerin', "Pearl! Pearl!" I can't sleep. It's drivin' me bats. Request permission to move to another bed somewhere else, sir.

GLANZ   *(Moving to the end of CHALKLEY's bed)*   We're afraid you're just going to have to put up with that. You probably have only a few more days here. *(Glances at the stricken CHALKLEY and speaks in an aside to BUDWINKLE)* Though quite frankly, sir, we don't think anyone's going to have to put up with it for long. With this man's hypertension we'd be prepared for congestive heart failure at any moment.

LINEWEAVER *(To* STANCIK, *with a leer)*   Pretty droopy today, dreamboat. Skin it back. Squeeze it. Milk it down.

GLANZ   Here is a very difficult case, with continuing copious discharge and serious involvement in the vas deferens and the epididymus. Look at those flecks of blood. The sulfas just do not seem to be in any way effective, so it's hard to say how long we'll have this patient on our hands. The root cause with this man Stancik, as it is with so many others, is a rampaging libido, along with a sexual history that staggers the mind. Stancik says he first indulged in intercourse at the age of nine—

STANCIK   *(Cheerfully)*   Age eight, sir.

GLANZ   Eight, then. And though now only twenty-four years old, he admits to carnal knowledge of nearly fifty women—

STANCIK   It was sixty, sir. I told you. Remember that list I made—

GLANZ   Sixty! Even more revealing! God! Sixty women, including the most depraved and debased streetwalkers in port cities from Boston to Seattle! *(His voice rises, tinged with indignation)* Is it any wonder that Nature takes ruthless revenge upon such licentiousness? Lineweaver, raise this man's dosage to a full gram of sulfathiozale every four hours.

LINEWEAVER   Aye-aye, sir.
     (They move on)

GLANZ   *(Notices* BUDWINKLE *making a grimace of disgust as they pass by* CLARK*'s bed)*   That rancid, pungent odor you smelled, sir, is characteristic of the late ulcerative stage of granuloma. Not much hope for that one, we're afraid. He was far advanced when he reported his condition. *(After*

inspecting MC DANIEL, *he halts at* MAGRUDER *'s bed*) And here
we have the syphilis we told you about. What's your
name again, boy?

MAGRUDER   Magruder, sir. Private Wallace M., five-four-
two-three-oh-seven, United States Marine Corps Reserve.

LINEWEAVER *(Leering)*   Not bad for a kiddie. Skin it back.
Squeeze it. Milk it down.

GLANZ   No apparent discharge. This would indicate an ab-
sence of gonorrhea. So much for the lesser disease. But as
for syphilis, Captain, his Wassermann is positively
stratospheric. Or—ha!—should we say, stratospherically
positive? Magruder, we want you to repeat in the pres-
ence of the Captain the information you gave us last
night. First, you say you have never at any time noticed
a chancre—a distinct ulcer or sore—on any of your private parts.

MAGRUDER   Yes, sir, that's right. Never.

GLANZ   Second, you have never been aware, in the last year
or so, of a measle-like rash spreading over large parts of
your body, and which might have been accompanied by
a feeling of illness, or headache or sore throat or nausea?

MAGRUDER   No, never, sir.

GLANZ   So you see, Captain, he denies any acquaintance
with the two symptoms which are an integral part of
early syphilis. *(To* MAGRUDER*)* You told us last night that
you were a college man.

MAGRUDER   I had a semester in college, sir.

GLANZ   You said you were studying English. That you
wanted to be a writer, or a poet, or some kind of scribbler.

MAGRUDER   Yes, sir, I've written some short stories. And I write poetry—I try to.

GLANZ   To be a writer requires a rather highly developed capacity for observation, does it not?

MAGRUDER   I imagine so, sir.

GLANZ   *Imagine?* You know perfectly well that it does! And you—a college man with literary ambitions, a man supposed to be observant, *trained* to be observant—you still can stand there and claim that you never once observed any of these symptoms and signs?

MAGRUDER   That's right, sir.

GLANZ   *(Shakes his head)*   A very likely story. *(To* BUDWINKLE *)* Last night, sir, when we made a cursory physical examination, we noticed something which further helped ratify our conviction of the presence of syphilis. *(Elaborately dons a rubber glove and takes* MAGRUDER *'s penis between his fingers)* As you can see, the boy is circumcised, which of course is no longer a rarity at all among those of the Gentile persuasion. What *is* your faith, by the way?

MAGRUDER   I'm a Presbyterian, sir.

GLANZ   And, one might add, a *backslider*, eh, Magruder? Now notice, Captain, the small, pink, raised scar on the ventral surface right behind the corona. To our own practiced eyes—if you'll pardon the personal allusion—it looks like nothing so much as the scar left by a venereal chancre.

MAGRUDER   But I told you, sir, I've had that little scar ever since I was a kid!

GLANZ   It's the same story he told us last night. The implication being, of course, that the scar must have been the result of a somewhat less than perfect removal of the foreskin. *(Chuckles)* Another sly evasion, we're afraid.

BUDWINKLE   Well, Doctor, as everyone has come to know, it all simmers down to the age-old dilemma of a physician and his diagnosis. On the one hand: the doctor, trying only to extract the truth from the patient in order that he may most effectively employ the sacred art of healing—to treat him and make him well. On the other hand: the patient, so often guilty and devious, trying to squirm away from the truth—in this case, no doubt, because the truth would reveal a history of hanky-panky that smells like bilge water in a Shanghai junk.

MAGRUDER   But, sir! I *have* had that scar since I was a child! Ever since I began—well, *looking* at myself down there, I saw that scar! I tell you, sir, you've *got* to believe me— I've never had a *sore*—that thing you call a chancre— there *ever!*

GLANZ   Magruder, let us tell you something. Years of research by dedicated scientists have not produced our superb blood flocculation tests—the Wassermann and the Kahn—with the idea in mind that they might be discredited by some gossamer boyish fantasy. For the moment, in your case, we assume as fact the one-time presence of a chancre, just as we assume the present existence in you of syphilis.

BUDWINKLE   For heaven's sake, man, syphilis is a highly infectious disease! Belay all this guff! You can't be so indecent as to hold in callous disregard the lives of others —your fellow marines here who run the risk of being contaminated by you! In the name of God, have a little bit more simple decency!

GLANZ   Lineweaver, see that Magruder here uses the syphilitics' toilet and the syphilitics' washbasin. And also his eating utensils and tray will be specially sterilized and segregated from those of the other patients. (*To* BUDWINKLE) And now, sir, we want very much for you to see our laboratory. It's new and it's nifty.
(*They exit stage right*)

MAGRUDER   God! (*Sits on the end of his bed, head in hands, a picture of despair*) Ah, God!

LINEWEAVER   O.K., guys, you can use the head! Chow down in the mess hall in fifteen minutes!
(*Except for the two gravely sick men, and also* MAGRUDER *and* SCHWARTZ, *the patients grab towels and shaving gear and begin to straggle offstage, left*)

STANCIK   You lucky dog, Dadario. You'll be outa here next weekend. Tell me, what are you gonna do first? Give me three guesses.

DADARIO   No, I'll *tell* you what I'm goin' to do. I'm goin' to get a three-day pass and go to Savannah. Then I'm goin' to go to one of those seafood restaurants downtown and have a big meal of fried shrimp. Then I'm goin' to get myself started on a serious whiskey-drink all around town—

STANCIK   And then you're goin' to pick you up a broad, one of them sweet little Dixieland honeypots—

DADARIO   *No*, Stancik, for once in my life, for one single time in my life, I'm not goin' to get laid. I'm just goin' to sit there drinkin' whiskey, and I'm goin' to think of how it was back there in the clap shack, and I'll be thinkin' of you and that big, ugly, leakin' joint of yours, and for once in my life I'm goin' to be as pure as the first violet that blooms in the springtime. That's *all!*

(They exit, stage left)

MAGRUDER *(To himself)* You'd think that—something! *(Strikes his forehead in anguish)* Ah, Jesus! No!

SCHWARTZ *(He is sitting nearby)* I suggest you try to stay calm. Guys first come into this place and they panic. It's almost like a state of shock. You should stay calm. What you've got maybe can be cured, when they find out how far it's gone, and so on. I know a little something about it. I'm a hospital corpsman—O.K., a sick hospital corpsman—but I've seen plenty of guys cured for what you've got. It depends on how far it's gone.

> *(As* SCHWARTZ *speaks,* LINEWEAVER *quietly takes* CHALK-LEY*'s blood pressure, then moves to* CLARK*'s bedside, where, donning a surgical mask, he pulls back the sheets to expose* CLARK*'s inguinal—groin—area and gives him a hypodermic injection. Pulling back the sheets releases the full effect of the morbid odor, and both* MAGRUDER *and* SCHWARTZ *react to it,* MAGRUDER *violently)*

MAGRUDER What's that stink, Schwartz?

SCHWARTZ Clark. He's a mean one, that ni—oh, I almost said *nigger.* I never like to use that word. You know, I'm of an oppressed minority myself. But this nigger is *evil.* I think he's also half-crazy. He's dying. That smell. I've almost gotten used to it.

MAGRUDER What are you in here for?

SCHWARTZ Tuberculosis of the kidney, they think I have. A fuckin' awful disease. I've been here a long time. For me they don't have much of a cure, if that's what's wrong with me. At least for you they've got Dr. Ehrlich's Magic Bullet. And that works fine a lot of times, if what you've got hasn't progressed too far. That's why you should try to stay calm.

MAGRUDER   What's Dr. Ehrlich's Magic Bullet?

SCHWARTZ   You mean you never saw that movie about Dr. Ehrlich's Magic Bullet? Edward G. Robinson was the star of it. A hell of a movie! I remember I saw it—

MAGRUDER   *(Impatiently)* But the cure. What about the cure?

SCHWARTZ   The Magic Bullet? What he invented was some kind of chemical compound. Made out of arsenic or mercury, something like that. It's called 606. That's because it took Edward G. Robinson six hundred and six experiments before he found a drug that would work.

MAGRUDER   Well, how *does* it work?

SCHWARTZ   I don't know the exact way it's done. But this guy who was last here—this marine with syphilis who was here last month—they took him away to the hospital up at Bethesda. They said they were going to give him hypodermic injections for fifteen months.

MAGRUDER   God! Fifteen months. That's forever.

SCHWARTZ   Well, it beats dying. Almost anything beats dying.

MAGRUDER   *(After a long silence, rises to his feet)* You know, it's funny, Schwartz—I don't feel sick. I feel so well! And to think *(Pauses)* to think that one reason I joined the Marine Corps was so that I'd stop worrying about my health. I mean, as a civilian I was always worried about *some* disease—like I was going to get cancer. Or T.B. Christ, T.B.! Somebody would cough in my face and all day long I'd brood about it, thinking they'd given me T.B. Or arthritis! I'd get a charley horse in swimming, and then I'd forget about it, and the next day I'd wake up in bed and feel the pain in my leg and say to myself, "Shit! I've got arthritis." Once I was sure I had an incurable growth in my neck, and I finally got up enough courage to go to the doctor, and he felt it and told me it was just one of my ligaments. But I thought I would get over that, being a marine, running around and marching and doing push-ups and so on. Only, I become a marine and what happens? I find out I've got *syphilis.* The most positive Wassermann in the history of the United States Marine Corps! Christ, I've got these millions of germs *swarming* inside me—

SCHWARTZ   Spirochetes.

MAGRUDER   What did you say?

SCHWARTZ   Not *germs* inside you. Fuckin' *spirochetes.* That's what they're called. I've seen them in a microscope.

MAGRUDER   What's the difference?

SCHWARTZ   Germs look like—well, *germs.* Little rods and balls and globs and such. Syphilis spirochetes look like tiny little fuckin' corkscrews.

MAGRUDER *(With a small shudder)*   Jesus! Corkscrews! Billions of them!

SCHWARTZ   That's right. Billions of them. That's what makes syphilis different.

MAGRUDER   But Schwartz, listen, I *couldn't* have gotten syphilis! Because I—it's impossible! *(Pauses)* Well, I'm not really a virgin. I have had women—*two* of them. But they —no! I mean, I must have picked it up from a toilet seat or something.

LINEWEAVER *(Approaches, holding a white robe, and sarcastically picks up on* MAGRUDER*'s last line)*   Ho! Ho! Ho! A toilet seat! That's the oldest joke in the book, dopey. You couldn't get what you've got from a toilet seat if you slept with one every night for a year.

MAGRUDER   Then I must have gotten it in some mess hall or someplace, where the dishes and silver and things weren't washed properly—

LINEWEAVER   Wally, let me give you some good advice. Stop blaming inanimate objects for your problems. Syphilis is contracted in one way—through sex-u-al in-ter-course. Accept the fact that you're a very fancy fornicator —there's hardly any shame in that, after all—and that what happened to you could have happened to any dedicated whoremonger.

MAGRUDER   But that's just the point, don't you see? If I were some—what you call fancy fornicator, I'd understand! But I—

LINEWEAVER   *(Ignoring his words)*   You'll be using this robe instead of the one you're wearing. As you can see, it has a yellow "S" stitched to the breast, to identify your disease.

MAGRUDER   I can't wear that! Jesus, it's like—it's like *The Scarlet Letter!*

LINEWEAVER   *(Insistently)*   Yes, I think you *will* wear it, Wally. Dr. Glanz's rules.

MAGRUDER   When do I have to wear it?

LINEWEAVER   All the time on the ward, and whenever you go anywhere else in the hospital—to the mess hall, say, or to the movies, or the library.

MAGRUDER   *(Indignantly)*   Maybe you should give me a bell to ring, too! Like some—like some *leper!*

LINEWEAVER   Another thing. When you go to the head, you must use the toilet on the extreme right. It's plainly marked with a yellow "S," just like the washbasin you have to use.

MAGRUDER   If you say you can't pick it up from a toilet seat, why all the fuss about giving me a special one?

LINEWEAVER   It's simply a matter of *order*—so you'll get used to your new status.

MAGRUDER   I'll never get used to my new status. Never!

LINEWEAVER   Don't look so *glum*, Wally! After all, the clap patients have *their* separate facilities. We just don't want to mix up the gonococci with the spirochetes. A matter of order, that's all.

MAGRUDER   *(Looking at the letter on the robe)*   "S." It's yellow. A particularly repulsive shade of yellow. *(Turns to* SCHWARTZ*)* Why yellow? It makes me feel like—
        (He halts)

SCHWARTZ   Yes, Wally?
        (He exchanges a significant look with MAGRUDER*)*

MAGRUDER   *(Puts on the robe)*   Yes! Exactly! *(Strikes his forehead)* God almighty!

LINEWEAVER   *(As* DR. GLANZ *and* CAPTAIN BUDWINKLE *return from stage right)*   Attention on deck!
        *(*MAGRUDER *and* SCHWARTZ *stand at attention as the two officers pass through the ward)*

BUDWINKLE   A splendid lab, Dr. Glanz, perfectly splendid. Great little gadgets! I especially am taken by those Kraft-Stekel monoprecipitators. *(Chuckles)* I'll bet they set the Navy back a pretty penny.

GLANZ *(Also chuckles appreciatively)*   In the neighborhood of six of the "big bills," we should say, sir.

> *(As they talk, the other patients—who have been at their morning ablutions—straggle back onstage. At this moment* CHALKLEY *gives a loud, agonized moan from his bed.* LINE-WEAVER *rushes to his side, scrutinizes his face closely as he feels the man's pulse. He then hurries to the door at stage right)*

LINEWEAVER *(Shouts)*   Anderson! Smith! On the double here! Oxygen! *Adrenalin!* Hurry, I say! Chop-chop!

BUDWINKLE *(Oblivious of the pandemonium)*   It is too bad, however, Doctor, that you don't have a Banghart twin-speed pressure pump for reverse catheterizations. They're damned useful in a pinch.

GLANZ   Well, such a lack, sir, does indeed sorely trouble the heart of a deeply involved urologist like ourself. We hope and pray the Captain will put one on order.

> *(While they have been talking, center stage,* LINEWEAVER *has run back to* CHALKLEY*'s side, closely followed now by two hospital corpsmen,* ANDERSON *and* SMITH, *who are bearing with them the lifesaving paraphernalia that* LINE-WEAVER *has called for. As the three corpsmen huddle around the stricken man and apply their various instruments, the two officers continue to talk)*

BUDWINKLE   I'll try, I'll try. Well, it was an illuminating tour, Doctor. Your ward is about as shipshape as such a pesthole can get, and I congratulate you.

GLANZ   Thank you, sir. We always try to do our best.

BUDWINKLE   Keep me closely posted on your two terminal cases. Also that boy with syphilis. I'd especially like to know what you'll dredge up out of *that* rat's nest.

(While BUDWINKLE *speaks,* SCHWARTZ *has drawn close to* CLARK*'s bed, and he and the recumbent Negro are gazing intently at the frenzied, quiet activity of the three men at* CHALKLEY*'s bedside)*

MAGRUDER *(In a panicky voice)* What's he dying of, Schwartz?

SCHWARTZ It's some kind of nephritis, a kidney disease.

GLANZ Aye-aye, sir. It shouldn't be too long before we've developed a most revealing sexual profile.

MAGRUDER Nephritis! *(Gives a shudder)* Jesus, you don't suppose it's contagious, do you? *(Backs away)* This place is a *charnel house!*

BUDWINKLE Thank you, Doctor! Smooth cruising! And keep up the good work!
(He exits stage right, while GLANZ, *basking in the praise, stands with his back to the tense episode on stage. The lights fade)*

Around noontime of the same day. The routine now is similar to that of the early morning. Except for the two bedridden patients, the occupants of the ward are clad in robes. A couple loll about on their beds. Others sit on chairs reading, for the most part comic books. A portable radio plays "Frenesi" and other tunes of the swing music era. One or two of the patients—including MA-GRUDER, whose bed is next to CLARK's—are reading or writing letters. ANDERSON, a hospital corpsman, sits attentively next to CHALKLEY's bed, occasionally administering oxygen and monitoring the condition of the critically ill patient. As they attend to their various activities, a personage in the vestments of a CATHOLIC CHAPLAIN enters stage left and approaches LINEWEAVER, who has entered from stage right and who at this moment is hovering over CHALKLEY's bed. The CHAPLAIN is accompanied by a young assistant bearing the equipment used in the last rites of the Church.

CHAPLAIN *(To LINEWEAVER)* I was told that there was a man here who required the last rites.

LINEWEAVER I don't think so, sir.

CHAPLAIN *(Looking somberly at CHALKLEY)* Why? This man is clearly gravely ill.

LINEWEAVER Well, *that's* for sure, sir. He's in a coma. He couldn't be any sicker.

CHAPLAIN *(Moving forward)* Then I shall certainly administer extreme unction.

LINEWEAVER But, sir, the man's a Baptist.

CHAPLAIN He couldn't be a Baptist.

LINEWEAVER Pardon me, sir, but he is. He told me. Besides, it's on his dog tags. "P" for Protestant.

CHAPLAIN Listen, this is impossible. I received a message from regimental headquarters saying that a Catholic will be dying on B Ward.

LINEWEAVER But, sir, this is D Ward.

CHAPLAIN You mean, this is not B for Baker Ward?

LINEWEAVER No, sir. D for Dog Ward.

CHAPLAIN D for Dog?

LINEWEAVER Yessir. B Ward's orthopedic.

CHAPLAIN Then what's this?

LINEWEAVER Urological and venereal.

CHAPLAIN Urological and venereal? *(Shudders)* Heavens! *(To the* ASSISTANT, *briskly)* Come along, Wilkins! Quickly! Quickly!
> *(He hurries offstage left and exits, trailed by the* ASSISTANT *with his equipment. At extreme stage left is the bed of a young marine named* McDANIEL, *who has been avidly rereading the letter he has just received. He rises suddenly from his chair, and his voice arrests the attention of the other patients)*

McDANIEL I don't believe it! I just don't believe it!

DADARIO   What happened, McDaniel? You gettin' surveyed out of the service?

MCDANIEL   It's a letter—I mean a personal letter—from Rhonda Fleming's personal secretary!

STANCIK   What did Rhonda say, McDaniel? Does she want to blow you?

MCDANIEL   *(With real reproof)*   Cut it out, you creep! You're not fit to utter her name! *(Returns to the letter)* Listen to this. "Dear Davy: Like all screen stars, Miss Fleming receives hundreds of fan letters every day, and she could not possibly answer them herself. But you write her so often that she's terribly impressed, and she wanted me to send you this personal message. She thinks marines like you are the finest, cleanest, bravest boys in America, and she hopes you'll be thinking of her when you go overseas and slap that Jap. Sincerely yours . . ."
     (His voice trails off in awe)

STANCIK   I'll bet she'd shit if she knew you had the clap.

MCDANIEL   *(Advances angrily on STANCIK)*   Listen, you jerk, I've had just about enough out of you—

LINEWEAVER   *(Moves between them)*   Come, come, no roughhouse, boys! It's twelve o'clock. Time for chow! *(To all)* Chow down, you guys! All except you, Schwartz. You've got a stomach exam this afternoon.
     (The patients exit stage left, leaving MAGRUDER sitting on the chair by his bed, SCHWARTZ near him. The HOSPITAL CORPSMEN leave the bedside of CHALKLEY, who lies breathing under oxygen. LINEWEAVER looks back from extreme stage left)

LINEWEAVER   No chow for you, sonny boy?

MAGRUDER   No, I'm—I just don't seem to have any appetite. I'll just stay here, if it's O.K.

LINEWEAVER *(Rather sympathetically)*:   Sure, Wally. I understand. Lots of guys lose their appetite when they first come in here. You'll get it back.
>   (LINEWEAVER *exits.* MAGRUDER *sits reading one of the letters for a moment.* CLARK, *silent and propped against the pillows, gazes with the listlessness of one who is very sick at* MAGRUDER *and* SCHWARTZ)

SCHWARTZ *(His voice touched with envy and admiration)*   You got a lot of letters.

MAGRUDER *(Self-deprecatingly)*   Oh—well, yes, I guess I did. Five. I guess that's a lot for one day.

SCHWARTZ   I only got one, but at least I get one almost every day. From my wife. That's something. It makes you feel less lonesome. Who'd you get your letters from?

MAGRUDER   My girl, she's in my home town in Virginia. Sometimes she writes me a couple times—more!—maybe three times a day. Mainly she writes me about the books she's been reading. She's very big on poetry, like I am.

SCHWARTZ   She a blonde or brunette?

MAGRUDER   Sort of in between, I guess you'd say. Chestnut brown, would that be the right description? Yeah, chestnut brown.

SCHWARTZ   Has she got a nice build?

MAGRUDER *(With feeling)*   She's got *everything.*

SCHWARTZ   I wish my wife had everything. Her face, it's nice. It looks a little like—well, she looks a little bit like Ava Gardner. But the rest of her—the build—it's gone to fat. It's a shame. *(Pauses)* Chestnut brown. I like that color. I like poetry, too.

MAGRUDER *(With spirit)*   You do? What poets have you read?

SCHWARTZ   Oh, I don't read much poetry. I read books though. Constructive books. *(Gestures at two books nearby)* Things that are valuable and you can really get your teeth into.

MAGRUDER   What books are they?

SCHWARTZ   Well, this one is called *How To Manage a Pet Shop.* After the war I'm going to buy a pet shop. I like animals—dogs, cats, birds, turtles, snakes even. I'd love to have a pet shop. Then this other book is called *(Reading title) Tolerance for Others, or How to Develop Human Compassion,* by Rabbi Max Weinberg of Temple Rodef Sholem, Cincinnati, Ohio. What a book! What a fuckin' marvelous book!

MAGRUDER   It sounds interesting. Impressive. What's it all about?

SCHWARTZ   Well, mainly it's about suffering.

MAGRUDER   How do you mean?

SCHWARTZ   Well, he tells about how in my *(Hesitates)*—in my *ethnic,* our people have borne unspeakable oppression for many thousands of years. Listen—*(Begins to read)* "Persecuted, enslaved, the *poor* victims of—"

CLARK *(Interrupting)*   Poor! Hee-hee! Poor! Dat do grab my black ass! *Rich,* you means! De Jew ain't poor, de Jew is *rich!* De Jew is rich like de First National Bank of Memphis. De Jew is *poor?* Hee-hee! Dat is plain, ordinary *mu-ule* shit! Ole Man Klein in my hometown of Bolivar, Tennessee, dat Jew so rich he pee into a solid gold pisspot. Dat "poor" jive! Dat *do* grab my ass!

(Falls back with a sigh)

SCHWARTZ *(With great patience)* Just ignore that nigger. He's evil, that one. Anyway, to answer your question further, what he says in this book, *Tolerance for Others*, is that since the Jewish people have endured so much suffering, they must comprehend the suffering of others and be what he calls the standard bearers in the march for human compassion. *(Pauses, reads)* "There is one lesson for humanity: people must love one another."

CLARK Hee-hee! Dat is *mule shit!*

MAGRUDER *(After a pause)* Well, what do you mean about liking poetry, Schwartz?

SCHWARTZ What I mean by liking it is, I like the idea of poetry *being* there—for people who like it.

MAGRUDER Then didn't you ever read any poetry?

SCHWARTZ Sure. I recited a poem out loud when I graduated from high school. I won a prize for it, too! *(Glumly, after a pause)* A framed picture of the superintendent of the Board of Education.

MAGRUDER What was the poem?

SCHWARTZ "Crossing the Bar," by Tennyson. I still know it by heart. *(Pauses)* "Sunset and evening star, and one clear call for me. And may there be no moaning at the bar, when I put out to sea . . ." *(Pauses, reflects)* That's beautiful poetry, isn't it? And sad. It's about dying.

MAGRUDER Well, yes. *(Hesitantly)* It *is* beautiful, but—but there's other poetry that does so much more to me. I mean, have you ever read T.S. Eliot?

CLARK T.S. Eliot. Eliot, *T.S.* Dat means *tough shit* for Eliot. Tee-hee!

SCHWARTZ   Shut up! Go on, Wally. Who is this poet?

MAGRUDER   T.S. Eliot. He's a great poet. He's fantastic! And then there's Emily Dickinson, and Hart Crane, and Wallace Stevens. Stevens! He writes pure music! There's this passage of his—it's about dying, too—that goes like this: "The body dies; the body's beauty lives . . . So evenings die . . . in their green going, a wave . . . interminably flowing." *(Pauses)* And you want to know something, Schwartz? This guy Stevens is the vice-president of an insurance company up in Hartford, Connecticut!

SCHWARTZ   *(Ruminatively)* "The body dies; the body's beauty lives." That's *good*. He writes good poetry. And you say he's in insurance? What did you say his name is —Eliot?

MAGRUDER   Stevens. Wallace Stevens. I'd give anything to be able to write lines of poetry like that.

SCHWARTZ   "The body dies; the body's beauty lives." *(Long pause)* They're running a stomach test on me this afternoon. On top of my kidney thing, Dr. Glanz thinks I might have developed some kind of an ulcer.

MAGRUDER   God, I'm sorry about that.

SCHWARTZ   You can't win! You have T.B. of the kidney and you worry about that until you get an ulcer. Now I'm worried about my ulcer.

CLARK   *(He has been gazing at* MAGRUDER *and* SCHWARTZ, *and now his sudden giggle startles them again)* Hee-hee! *(There is a sick lassitude in his laugh, and his voice is spiritless, enervated)* Hee-hee! Dat poetry jive! Dat is some kind of funny! You white boys so full of shit hit runnin' clean out yo' ears.

MAGRUDER   What's *wrong* with him?

SCHWARTZ   He's a mean one, that *schwarze*. I think he's half out of his mind. It's that sickness of his.

CLARK   Ain't never listened to such dumb, low-down white boys' *mule shit* in all my life. Hee-hee! Dat is sho some kind of funny. *(Rises slowly on his elbow)* Po-etry! Dat do grab my black ass!

MAGRUDER *(Placatingly)*   Gee, I didn't mean—

SCHWARTZ   Don't pay any attention to him. He's a menace. Shut your face, Lorenzo! *(In an aside)* I've gotta have tolerance! *(In an unctuous tone)* Just try to sleep.

CLARK   Ain't studyin' about no sleep, Jew-boy.

SCHWARTZ   He's *filled* with hate. Once—before you came here—I had a visit from my wife. Only when she arrived I wasn't on the ward at the moment. Then when Clark saw her, he told her that I had died.

MAGRUDER   That's awful!

CLARK   De Man *(Gestures weakly to heaven)* de *Man* gwine shut *my* face soon enough. And I'll get sleep. And you too, Jew-boy. Because you and me—us gwine *die!*

SCHWARTZ *(Shudders)*   I can't stand it!

MAGRUDER   What's *wrong* with him?

CLARK *(To MAGRUDER)*   Likewise you dere too, white boy, you wid dat sy-philis. Hee! hee! Dey gwine carry you outa here in a wooden kee-mo-no.

SCHWARTZ   I'm goin' to get Lineweaver to shut him up. *(In a sudden rage)* You stink to heaven, Lorenzo! Fuck tolerance! Fuck you too, Lorenzo!

CLARK   I *do* stink and I *is* black, and I is po' as Job's turkey, and I isn't got any kinfolk to mou'n me to my grave. But one thing I does know is dat dere ain't no difference between a dead nigger and a dead Jew-boy when dey is both food for de worms. *Equal!*
(*Sinks back, depleted, breathing heavily*)

SCHWARTZ   Why do you hate so? (CLARK *does not reply*) I've never done a fuckin' thing to you! (*To* MAGRUDER) I've only tried to be friendly to him.

MAGRUDER   Maybe you're right. Maybe that sickness has gotten to his brain.

SCHWARTZ   I can't think of anything else. (*Suddenly* MA-GRUDER *leaps to his feet, standing rigidly erect at the end of his bed*) What's wrong?

MAGRUDER (*In great agitation*)   Jesus Christ, I feel like I've died and waked up in hell! This place is driving me ape-shit!

SCHWARTZ   Take it easy, Wally!
(*As* SCHWARTZ *attempts to calm him, a light goes up in* GLANZ'*s office, and* GLANZ *appears—this time garbed in a doctor's white jacket. Simultaneously,* LINEWEAVER *appears at extreme stage left*)

LINEWEAVER   Magruder! Dr. Glanz wants you for an examination.

SCHWARTZ (*To* MAGRUDER, *as he crosses the stage*)   Good luck, Wally.
(MAGRUDER *enters* GLANZ'*s office and stands at attention*)

MAGRUDER   Private Magruder, Wallace M., five-four-two-three-oh-seven, reporting as ordered, sir.

GLANZ (*Fiddles with papers, without looking up from the desk where he is seated*)   At ease, Magruder. Sit down. (MA-

GRUDER *takes a chair opposite the doctor, who continues to shuffle ostentatiously through his papers, then finally looks up)* We'll come directly to the point, Magruder. Despite the famous toilet-seat myth, syphilis is *always* contracted through sexual intercourse. Consequently, following a clinical examination such as you have already received, a thorough and meticulous history must be made of a patient's sexual activities. You understand the logic of this, do you not?

MAGRUDER Yes, sir.

GLANZ Very well. It is not our intention, today, to obtain from you this sexual profile in detail. That will come in due course. However, we do want to take the first preliminary steps. Let us then ask you this. With how many women have you had sexual congress?
    (Begins to make notes)

MAGRUDER In my entire life, sir?

GLANZ In your entire life.

MAGRUDER Two women, sir.

GLANZ *(After a long pause and a penetrating gaze)* Magruder, look at us. Look at us carefully. Can you do that?

MAGRUDER I am looking at you—at you all—carefully, sir.

GLANZ You see that we are a grown man of middle age, father of four children, medical training in Budapest, Guy's Hospital, London, University of Arkansas, member of the American Medical Association, fellow of the American College of Urological Surgeons, listed in *Who's Who in America*, a practitioner of the art of medicine for twenty-five years. You see before you a man of large experience, and we hope, at this late date, of some wisdom. No less and no more than any of our patients, we suffer. If you prick us, we too will say "Ouch." In short, you see a very deeply human human being. *(Pauses)* All the more reason, then, that we feel that we are endowed with insight. Therefore what you do *not* see, on the other hand, is an innocent. What you do *not* see, Magruder, is a sucker. You do not see a callow, gullible young intern eager to swallow any harebrained invention that might pass a patient's lips. Do you expect us then to believe that you have had intercourse with *only two* women?

MAGRUDER *(Emphatically)*   Yes, sir, because it's a fact.

GLANZ   Preposterous.

MAGRUDER   Well, sir, can't you see? There hasn't been enough time. I'm sorry! I'm just eighteen!

GLANZ   You're young, it's true, but most of those fellow marines of yours—no older than you and in your same fix —have confessed to relations with women by the *score*. Regrettably, there is no truth serum available to elicit the real facts from you. *(Sighs)* Though we are convinced that you lie, we have no alternative but to take you at your word. *(Pauses, gazes intently into* MAGRUDER*'s eyes)* Only two, you say. Just who were these—these females?

MAGRUDER   One of them was—*(He falters, embarrassed)* She was—

GLANZ   Come, come, Magruder. You must have no hesitancy about these matters. Can't you understand? We are recording these details so that we can try to *save your life!*

MAGRUDER   She was an older woman, sir.

GLANZ   An older woman. Would you mind telling us how many times you had physical contact with this older woman?

MAGRUDER   Once, sir. Only once.

GLANZ   All it *takes* is once. And the other—female. Who was she?

MAGRUDER   She's my—well, she's my *girl*, sir.

GLANZ   You speak of her in the present tense. We assume this means that you have recently had relations with this girl of yours, and/or continue to have such relations.

MAGRUDER   That's right, sir.

GLANZ   She's how old?

MAGRUDER   She's just my age, sir. Eighteen. Well, a bit younger. Seventeen-and-a-half.

GLANZ   May we ask how many times you have had sexual contact with this girl?

MAGRUDER   (*A long pause*)   Oh, gee, sir, I wouldn't know. I would have lost count. Many, many times. Maybe hundreds. I've been in love with her for two years or more.

GLANZ (*Arises and goes to one wall of the office, where he pulls down a huge chart or diagram, a grotesque cartoon which is clearly that of the human brain*)   Hundreds, eh, Magruder? We'd say you've got a pretty athletic little romance going there. (*Gestures toward chart*) Do you know what this is?

MAGRUDER   Well, sir, it looks like a kind of map, or medical chart or something, of the brain.

GLANZ   Precisely. A diagram of that grandest and most complex of organs, the human brain.

MAGRUDER   It certainly *looks* complex, sir.

GLANZ   *The brain*. It may be the most majestic creation of the deity. It is here that it originates, Magruder, the ineffable mystery of *thought*—that miraculous process which has allowed mankind to produce its real standouts: a

Henry Ford, say, or a musical prodigy like John Philip Sousa, or professional heroes in our own pantheon, like Rudolf Wachter, the father of bladder surgery. A noble machine, would you not agree?

MAGRUDER   Yes, sir.

GLANZ   Yet a machine subject to malfunction, to bugs, gremlins, to breakdown—like all machines. In short, a mechanism subject to *disease. (Pauses)* Magruder, did you ever hear of the word paresis?

MAGRUDER   No, sir.

GLANZ   You have no idea, then, what paresis means, or what the definition of paretic is?

MAGRUDER   No, I'm afraid I don't, sir.

GLANZ   To be paretic is to have paresis. Paresis in turn is a neurological form of syphilis which affects the brain.

MAGRUDER *(Anxiety in his voice now)*   How does it affect the brain, sir?

GLANZ *(Takes a pointer in hand)*   It creates an inflammatory process, known as meningoencephalitis. This inflammation may appear on any brain area but tends to localize *(Indicates with pointer)* here at the basal aspect. Or here at the frontal aspect.

MAGRUDER   Well, sir, what happens to someone when this takes place?

GLANZ   The patient becomes insane. *(Pauses)* Stark, raving mad. *(Long pause)* Loony as a dingbat.

MAGRUDER *(Gasps)*   Jesus! Sir.

GLANZ   Let us ask you something else, Magruder. Have you ever heard of locomotor ataxia?

MAGRUDER   No, sir. What's that?

GLANZ   Locomotor ataxia is another form of neurosyphilis.
It affects the posterior columns of the spinal cord *(Uses
pointer)* here, and certain cranial nerves, here and here,
including the optic nerve, here.

MAGRUDER   And what happens with this, sir?

GLANZ   The patient becomes unable to walk properly.
Then he goes blind. He also finally becomes hopelessly
paralyzed.

MAGRUDER   My God!
*(Begins, almost unconsciously, to feel himself, arms and
legs)*

GLANZ   It's a bitch of a disease, Magruder, we'll tell you.
*(Pauses, rolls the chart back up so that it snaps like a window
shade, sits down once again)* You may think that we have
shown you all this in order to alarm you, but we can
assure you that this has not been our intention.

MAGRUDER   I hope you'll pardon me for saying so, sir, but
it sure *does* alarm me. God—I'm alarmed!

GLANZ   We've done this not to alarm you but to shock you
into an awareness of the seriousness of your condition.
Also to impress upon you the necessity for perfect
honesty and candor on your part in any discussion the
two of us will have in regard to your sexual history. The
evidence now speaks for itself. You must have chosen to
ignore the early symptoms—the chancre and the rash.
Therefore we are forced inescapably to believe that you
have passed out of the primary and secondary stages of
syphilis and are now passing into the last—the tertiary
stage. While ordinarily the grave conditions I've de-
scribed to you take a number of years to develop, there
is a form of the disease which is not uncommon called

"galloping syphilis," in which the patient is quickly overwhelmed by paresis or locomotor ataxia, or both. It is *this* that we are concerned about in your case. *(Pauses)* Alas, also the possibility of—*(He shrugs)*

MAGRUDER *(In a real panic)*   Then doesn't this mean I'm going to *die?* Isn't that what you're saying, sir? That I'm going to get all these things you've been describing? Jesus, sir, isn't there any hope for me? Any at all!

GLANZ *(Disarmed for the first time, he softens a little bit and his voice loses some of its harshness)*   No, no, Magruder! Calm yourself, boy! There's no *certainty* in any of this!

MAGRUDER *(Almost in tears)*   But you make it sound so certain, sir! God, I don't want to go crazy! Get paralyzed, go blind! I'd rather *die!*

GLANZ   We insist that you calm yourself! We can understand this self-concern in you. It is normal of you to have this fear. But you must remember that we have drugs which are sometimes effective in arresting this disease. *(Smiles thinly)* Unless, of course, it has progressed *too far.*

MAGRUDER   Six-o-six? The Magic Bullet? Fifteen months of injections?

GLANZ   For a layman, you have a rare expertise, Magruder. Yes, that drug has been used with some success. Keep that in mind. We want you to leave this office in an optimistic mood. And now you're dismissed.

> (MAGRUDER, *weak and shaken, rises, does an about-face and walks toward the office door)*

GLANZ   Oh, Magruder.

MAGRUDER *(Abruptly turning)*   Sir?

GLANZ *(Raises the thumb of his right hand in a gesture of bonhomie and palship)*   Chin up, there!

(MAGRUDER *walks, shaken, dejectedly across the ward to the place by his bed.* SCHWARTZ *looks up from his book*)

SCHWARTZ   How did it go, Wally?

MAGRUDER   Terrible, Schwartz. Terrible! It couldn't have gone worse. (*Pauses, wondering*) I mean, that *Glanz!* He's, he's a—
(*He halts*)

SCHWARTZ   Don't let Dr. Glanz get *to* you like that, Wally. He's well-known for always wanting people to be sick. It's what's known as a personality quirk, I think.

MAGRUDER   (*Taking out of his footlocker a piece of writing paper and a fountain pen*)   Well, Schwartz, he *did* get to me. He did get to me, that son of a bitch!
(*He begins to write, and as he writes, for a minute or so a portable radio is heard, playing a strange mélange of hill-billy music, scraps of hit songs of the period, a brief insane passage from Bach's* St. Matthew Passion, *war reports from the Pacific, announcing huge marine casualties at Tarawa. Finally he breaks off writing, places pen and paper down and slowly rises to his feet. He is greatly agitated*)

SCHWARTZ   Writing to the little sweetheart, I'll bet. You hurt my conscience, Wally. I owe my wife a letter for over a week. (*With a look of revulsion,* MAGRUDER *tears the letter to pieces. At this,* SCHWARTZ *rises too*) What's wrong? Take it easy! Listen, don't panic!

MAGRUDER   (*Cries out in the direction of* GLANZ*'s office*)   You're not going to get *me*, Dr. Glanz! I'm not going to *die* in this stinking, misbegotten, low-down *kennel* of yours. You hear me, Dr. Glanz?

SCHWARTZ   Quiet, Wally! *Quiet!* You can't *do* that! If he ever heard you, he'd punish the whole ward! Quiet!

MAGRUDER *(Calmer now)*   But I can't *stand* this place! It's going to drive me absolutely crackers!

SCHWARTZ   You just have to have courage, Wally. Courage! Like Rabbi Weinberg says, the handmaiden of tolerance is *courage.*

CLARK *(Rising up on his elbow)*   Courage! Tee-hee! Dat is some kind of mule shit!

SCHWARTZ *(Turning in a rage)*   Shut up! God, you stink to-day! I can't stand the way you smell, it's worse than ever! Why don't you die? *(Wrings his hands, averting his eyes)* Forgive me. Tolerance!

CLARK *(Weakly)*   It ain't *me* dat stink so bad. *(Gestures in the direction of* CHALKLEY's *bed)* Why don't you take you a whiff of *him?* He *stone dead,* smellin' like a ole catfish all mornin'. *(Pauses)* Food for de worms. *Equal!*
  (His laughter dominates the scene. MAGRUDER, SCHWARTZ *and, more slowly, the other patients on the ward turn and gaze silently at* CHALKLEY's *inert form as the lights go down on the stage)*

Act Two

It is a week later, in the hour of the morning before reveille.
LINEWEAVER *is absent from his desk and most of the patients are*
asleep. MAGRUDER, *however, stirs slowly awake and sits on the edge*
of his bed. Soon SCHWARTZ *awakens too, and sits up erect in bed,*
yawning and stretching.

MAGRUDER   What time is it?

SCHWARTZ   It's a little after six. Reveille's in half an hour.
    (Yawns) I'm so tired! For some reason I couldn't sleep.

MAGRUDER *(Yawns too)*   Where's Lineweaver?

SCHWARTZ   I can't say for sure, but I suspect he's doping
    off. Asleep. He comes in from an all-night liberty and
    goes to sleep in the laboratory. Once one morning I
    peeked in there, and there he was—snoozing like a baby
    among the urine specimens and the Bunsen burners. Boy,
    if Dr. Glanz ever caught him at that!

MAGRUDER *(Yawns again, almost painfully)*   I couldn't really
    sleep either. Tossed and turned all night long, filled with
    these strange dreams.

SCHWARTZ   They must have been bad, Wally. You kept
    groaning and talking in your sleep. I couldn't understand
    anything you said—except one word. Ha! That was
    funny!

MAGRUDER What word did I say?

SCHWARTZ You know what you said? You said, "Vladivostok."

MAGRUDER "Vladivostok!" Why would I say a thing like that?

SCHWARTZ I don't know, Wally. Maybe it's because you were dreaming about it. Vladivostok, that's in Russia, isn't it? I mean it's so *far away* from *here!* It's probably what Rabbi Weinberg calls a wish-fulfillment dream. *(Reaches for the book)* You know, the Rabbi has an answer for almost any problem. Here, let me read you—

MAGRUDER No Rabbi this morning, Schwartz! No more Weinberg! Please! Jesus, I've got to get out of this place!

SCHWARTZ Take it easy, Wally. Take it easy. You're not the only one stuck in this fuckin' place!
    (Approaches MAGRUDER *as if to calm him, and then coughs)*

MAGRUDER Don't get too close, Schwartz. Get away!

SCHWARTZ *(Soothingly)* Wally, Wally, you can't catch my T.B. when I cough! It's in my *kidney!* Calm down now. Take it easy! Just get hold of yourself, Wally!

MAGRUDER *(In sudden, intense embarrassment)* I'm sorry, Schwartz. I really am. I'm ashamed of myself. Jesus, if I don't die of locomotor ataxia I'll die of hypochondria. *(Pauses)* But that's just it! You know, Schwartz, if I just had some *knowledge* I might be able to make it. *Knowledge* might make me able to get through this. I mean, for instance, I had another blood test yesterday. The idea scares me. I mean, I don't know anything about blood tests. I'm a medical idiot.

SCHWARTZ   You mean you really want to know *more* about what you've got? If you'll forgive me, Wally, I'd say that when it comes to syphilis, ignorance is bliss.

MAGRUDER   No, I want some information about this disease I've got. Something that might show me what to look for —what symptoms, what signs! Some information that could even give me a little hope—like knowing that the disease might have, well, *stabilized* itself and maybe wasn't going to get any worse. I try to worm a little knowledge out of Dr. Glanz, but I can't even get a word of consolation from him, much less any facts. All he seems to care about is taking my what he calls sexual profile. Jesus, I forgot! I've got another one of those sexual profile sessions with him today. What a *jerk!*

SCHWARTZ   Yes, sir, I'll have to agree to one thing. That Dr. Glanz is a tough cookie.

MAGRUDER   *(In a sudden fury)*   That's an understatement if I ever heard one, Schwartz! Tough cookie! Why, some-times I think he's hardly made of flesh! I thought doctors were supposed to make you feel *better*, not make you feel like some worm, some worthless piece of *slime!* He's in-credible! He's a *troglodyte!*

SCHWARTZ   But, you know, I get to thinking: sometimes doctors have to *act* hard, tough. To protect themselves. They see so much pain, so much suffering. Actually, I'll bet Dr. Glanz is—well, very tolerant and also deeply human.

MAGRUDER   Deeply human! For God's sake, that's what *he* said! Don't make me puke, Schwartz! Tolerant? Stop it! Your Jewish compassion is showing! He's a pluperfect prick! I'd like to kick him in the teeth! *(Pauses)* Yet he scares me. That I must admit.

SCHWARTZ *(Suddenly inspired)*   Hey, I got an idea!

MAGRUDER   An idea about what?

SCHWARTZ   About that knowledge—that information you were talking about.

MAGRUDER   What do you mean?

SCHWARTZ   Books! In Dr. Glanz's office. There are all sorts of textbooks on your disease that could tell you everything you want to know.

MAGRUDER   Yeah, but, Schwartz, since when did doctors start distributing medical textbooks to sick people?

SCHWARTZ *(His voice conspiratorial now)*   No, I don't mean that. I mean we just *borrow* a book for a little while. *(Gets out of bed)* Look, the office is open. Lineweaver's asleep. It'll be easy as pie, Wally!
   (Begins to move toward the office)

MAGRUDER   Wait, Schwartz, you'd better not! You'll get ten years in the Portsmouth brig if Lineweaver or someone catches you stealing one of those books!

SCHWARTZ *(Insistently)*   He'll never miss it if I take it just for a little while. I'll put it back right away, sometime when he's not there. *(Heads toward the office in a hurried tiptoe past the sleeping patients)* Don't worry, Wally!
   (While SCHWARTZ exits, CLARK stirs in his bed. As on the earlier morning, we are made aware that the black man has been closely attending the previous conversation, silently listening to every word)

CLARK *(His voice weak and strained as usual)*   How is de syphilis dis mawnin'?

MAGRUDER *(Truly startled)* WHAT!

CLARK Hush, man! You gwine rouse up de whole hospital. How come you jump like dat?
> *(At stage left, in* GLANZ*'s office,* SCHWARTZ *takes a book from a shelf and begins to read, underlining certain passages with a pencil)*

MAGRUDER *(Recovering himself)* You startled me! I mean— well, it's the first thing you've said to me since the day I came into this place. I didn't expect it, that's all. I was startled.

CLARK *(Makes his cracked little laugh)* You looks better, white boy. Not so peak-ed roun' de jowls. I 'spect you might even live fo' a while—befo' you gits et up by dem *spiralkeets.*

MAGRUDER Don't make jokes like that. Jokes about *that*— in this place—they're not funny. *(Turns away)* You might as well get this straight: I'm not going to take any shit off you, Lorenzo. I'm not going to be another Schwartz. I'm not going to be another scapegoat for your misery.

CLARK No, listen, white boy, I wants to tell you somethin'. *(Halts, then continues to speak laboriously)* I *likes* you, I truly likes you—

MAGRUDER I don't want you to like me! *(Resentfully)* Stay off my back, Lorenzo! Leave me the fuck alone!

CLARK But I *does* like you! Likewise, I does *not* like de Jew-boy. I likes you all right. You wants to know why?

MAGRUDER *(Still seething)* Why, for God's sake?

CLARK Because you is a *Southren* boy. I is Southren too. Born and reared in Bolivar, Tennessee. Us Southren boys got to stick together. Born together. Die together. Dat's *equality.*

MAGRUDER   It's a pile of crap, if you want to know the truth, Lorenzo. Why do you hate Schwartz so much? Because he's Jewish?

CLARK   Because he a Jew-boy. *Yas!* An' because he afraid to believe he gwine to die. You an' me—us Southren boys —us *knows* we gwine die. Jew-boy, he gwine die too. He jus' skeered to own up to de nachel-born truth.

MAGRUDER   *(Angrily)*   What do you mean! He knows the truth. Schwartz is very sick. He's got advanced tuberculosis of the kidney. Every time he goes to the head, he pisses blood. He's *gravely ill* and he's terrified—like the rest of us. He doesn't want to die either. The only reason I can figure out why you hate him so is because he's Jewish. Why do you hate Jews like you do? Because they crucified Christ?

CLARK   No, man, because dey crucified de niggers. Ever hear tell of Ole Man Klein in my hometown of Bolivar, Tennessee? Mr. Samuel Klein who owned de Shoprite Department Sto'? My *daddy* owed Mr. Samuel Klein for ev'y blessed thing he had—owed fo' de raddio, 'frigerator, ten-piece suit of furniture in de front room, an' a fo'-foot picture of de Last Supper dat shined like de rainbow. Den dat year de cotton crop failed, and Daddy couldn't pay de 'stallments, and Mr. Samuel Klein he done *reclaim* ev'y stick, an' lef' dat house picked clean as a bone. *(Pauses)* Dat is de Jew *way!* Dat is de Jew way of skinnin' de black man's hide.

(He falls back exhausted)

MAGRUDER   But listen, Lorenzo, it's not just the Jews who've skinned the niggers, it's been *everyone!* I mean, sure, I believe your story about this man Klein, but what about the other white people? What *they've* done to colored people! I mean the Presbyterians, the Methodists, the Baptists—

LINEWEAVER *(Enters, sleepy-looking and somewhat disheveled, from stage right, picking up on* MAGRUDER *'s last line in a singsong litany)* The Congregationalists, the Episcopalians, the Mormons, the Moravians, the Seventh Day Adventists—well, what *are* you two doing up so early, deep in your metaphysics? *(Loudly, to the ward at large)* All right, you gyrenes, first call! Out of those sacks in five minutes!
(The patients begin to groan and stir)

MAGRUDER *(There is an edge of compassion in his voice, as if he is trying to cope with or understand the irrationality of this Negro)* Can't you see how wrong and stupid it is of you to feel this way? It's a tough spot we're all in here. We're all in a terrible situation. Why don't you try to like Schwartz too, Lorenzo? It won't do any of us any good if you keep on storing up this unreasonable hatred. Hatred for someone who's done you not the slightest bit of harm.

CLARK *(Feebly but with passion)* I'll like de Jew boy. I *will* like him! I'll like him on de day dat de Lawd makes roses bloom in a pig's asshole.
*(*MAGRUDER *makes a silent gesture of hopelessness and disgust)*

LINEWEAVER *(Intercepts* SCHWARTZ *with a book, which the latter tries at first to conceal, then decides to bluff it out)* Good morning, Schwartz! You look chipper today. *(Puts his hand on* SCHWARTZ *'s brow)* Fever down a little. Good. Stick out the old tongue. *(Inspects his tongue)* Beautiful tongue. What are you doing up so early?

SCHWARTZ   I couldn't sleep. I went into the head to read my book.

LINEWEAVER *(Merely curious)*   Yeah? What are you reading these days?

SCHWARTZ   It's a Jewish book. It's called *Mazeltov*. It's a kind of a Jewish cookbook.

LINEWEAVER *(Amiably pats* SCHWARTZ *'s arm and moves off to his desk, stage left)*   Getting pretty fed up with the chow, huh, Schwartz? Well, I don't blame you. The food they give you guys I wouldn't feed to Captain Budwinkle.
     (Winces slightly with his daring little jest. He then picks up some papers and charts from his desk and exits stage left. Now as the patients slowly rouse themselves, MAGRUDER *and* SCHWARTZ *sit on their adjacent beds and consult the book which has been appropriated)*

SCHWARTZ   Look, it's the biggest book I could find on syphilis. Also, it's got the longest title.

MAGRUDER   What's it called?

SCHWARTZ   *"The Complete Diagnostic and Therapeutic Source Book on Syphilis: A Guide to the Detection and Treatment of Syphilis, Acquired and Congenital; including Early Syphilis, both Primary and Secondary; Latent Syphilis, Early and Late; Late Syphilis; Cardiovascular Syphilis; Neurosyphilis; Meningovascular Syphilis; Locomotor Ataxia; and General Paresis.* Compiled by Martin J. McAfee, M.D., Isador Davidoff, M.D., Charles P. Dixon—"

MAGRUDER   Never mind who wrote it, Schwartz. What does it say? Especially what does it say about paresis? And locomotor ataxia? Those are two things I want to know most about.

SCHWARTZ *(An air of strained good humor in his voice)* Oh, I've got good news for you about them, Wally. Very good news indeed! *(Leafs through the index)* I would think things look very optimistic.

MAGRUDER Optimistic? How do you mean?

SCHWARTZ *(Refers to the book)* Well, get this—under "Locomotor Ataxia." In the part that talks about the prognosis. Get this. It says: "In about fifty percent of cases the disease becomes *stationary;* in the rest it progresses." There! Doesn't that make you optimistic?

MAGRUDER *(Reflects)* No, for God's sake! Why *should* it make me optimistic?

SCHWARTZ At least you've got a fifty-fifty chance of it not getting any worse.

MAGRUDER Oh, Jesus, yes, Schwartz, that makes me happy. Delirious! Why don't we break open a bottle of champagne? *(Puts his head in his hands)* Tell me some more.

SCHWARTZ Another very good piece of news. Listen. "Early, vigorous treatment improves the prognosis." There, that should make you feel better!

MAGRUDER *(Looks up)* But that's just the *point*, don't you see? How in God's name do I know—with me—if it's early? Like Dr. Glanz said, it may be already too *late*.

SCHWARTZ Well, that is true, Wally. That's something I suppose you just have to face. A fifty-fifty chance, though —it's not too bad. Not bad at all.

MAGRUDER O.K., let's say that I get all the symptoms tomorrow, but I'm lucky and it becomes stationary and doesn't progress. Tell me the good news.

SCHWARTZ *(Afraid of the dire revelation, hesitates)* Oh, Wally—

MAGRUDER   Read it, Schwartz, damn it! I'm not afraid to know. Go ahead! Read! What *happens* when I get locomotor ataxia?

SCHWARTZ *(Reads with reluctant slowness)* "Inability to move in the dark or to maintain equilibrium with the eyes shut —Romberg's sign—is noticed. Walking becomes unsteady, and the characteristic staggering gait appears. The patient walks with legs apart, head bent forward, eyes fixed on the ground. Leg movements are excessive, the foot being thrown out high and the heel coming down sharply in a slapping gait." *(As* SCHWARTZ *reads,* MAGRUDER *compulsively and with a fanatical glint in his eye begins to ape these symptoms, rising and duplicating the leg and foot movements in the space between the beds)* "Sudden stopping or quick turning causes staggering and sometimes a fall. Canes are necessary until all locomotion becomes impossible—at which point the patient often lapses into other manifestations such as incontinence, blindness, impotence and paralysis."

MAGRUDER *(Ceases his pantomime and sinks onto the edge of the bed)* Christ on a fucking crutch!

SCHWARTZ   Get this, though, Wally! It then says this: "Locomotor ataxia itself almost never causes death." Did you hear that? "Almost never causes death." Then *this:* "Many patients have lived twenty or twenty-five years or even longer."

MAGRUDER   Twenty-five years in bed—pissing in my pajamas, paralyzed, impotent and blind.
        (He and SCHWARTZ *stare wordlessly at each other as* LINEWEAVER *enters at stage left)*

LINEWEAVER (*Strides across the ward*)   Last call, boys! Drop your cocks and grab your socks! Hit the deck! Up and at 'em, gyrenes! Big treat in the mess hall this morning! Your choice of Post Toasties, Rice Krispies, or Wheaties, the Breakfast of Champions! Short-arm inspection in *pre*cisely ten minutes! (*Turns to* DADARIO) I'm going to miss you, Dadario. I'm going to miss the thrill of seeing that sensational tool of yours every day in the rosy dawn.
> (DADARIO, *alone among the others this morning, has donned the khaki uniform of a marine private, and is preparing to leave with his sea-bag*)

DADARIO   I'm goin' to miss you too, Lineweaver. You've been just a darling through it all.

LINEWEAVER (*To the patients*)   Say goodbye to Dadario, guys! Say farewell to a free man! (*A handful of the patients bid him goodbye in their various fashions. He then moves to the door, stage left, grinning, making a "V" for victory sign.* LINE-WEAVER *again addresses the ward at large*) There he goes, lads. Fit as a fiddle! Walking testimonial to the miracle of the healing sciences, of the triumph of Hygeia over the accursed gonococcus. As Dadario goes, so, in the fruition of time, shall ye all go!

MAGRUDER (*Watches* DADARIO *and* LINEWEAVER *exit, the latter going into the office to consult with* DR. GLANZ, *who has just arrived*)   I wish there was some way I was able to believe that. (*Turns back to* SCHWARTZ) What's the book say about paresis, Schwartz? That's the one that really bothers me. Paralysis, to go blind—that's all bad enough, but *insanity*—
> (*He breaks off with a shudder*)

SCHWARTZ   Very good news about paresis, Wally! Excellent news! (*Pauses, struggling to maintain his dauntless opti-*

mism) Maybe not so good news as with locomotor, but it still gives room for plenty of hope.

MAGRUDER   Like what?

SCHWARTZ   Well, listen. "Infrequently, remissions may occur to the extent of the patient being able to resume his occupation." There, how about that? You may get a remission. That's almost the same as being cured.

MAGRUDER   But didn't it say "infrequently"?

SCHWARTZ   Yes, it did.

MAGRUDER   Don't you know what infrequently means?

SCHWARTZ   Sure. Not frequent.

MAGRUDER   You think that's good news, then?

SCHWARTZ   Well, Wally, it's better than "never."

MAGRUDER *(Groans)*   What does it say about the symptoms?

SCHWARTZ *(Again hesitant)*   Wally, *Wally!* What's the point in all this? It's so painful. It's like picking at sores—

MAGRUDER   Go ahead and read it, Schwartz. Please! I'd rather know than not know.

SCHWARTZ *(Begins to read)*   "Most often the initial mental symptoms consist of insidious changes in personality, such as cleanliness of clothing and body." (SCHWARTZ *glances at* MAGRUDER, *who rather nervously straightens his robe, smooths back his hair, and in an abstracted way begins to clean his nails)* "Delusions concerning his property, position, family, or personal attainments may appear. A common first sign is the patient's suspicion that people in general are intent upon stealing his money or other belongings. On the other hand, with boastfulness and grandiosity he may believe himself a potentate or deity, the possessor of priceless jewelry, beautiful women, and fabulous wealth." *(Pauses and looks up)* I've never heard you boast about things like that, Wally. *(Half to himself)* Well, except maybe that girl— Anyway, you never talked like a potentate.

MAGRUDER *(Intensely nervous now)*   Not yet. Go on.

SCHWARTZ   "Serious defects in speech develop. In particular the consonants 'l' and 'r' are difficult for the paretic to enunciate. Hence he cannot readily articulate such test phrases as 'truly rural' . . . 'thirty-third artillery brigade' . . . 'around the rough and rugged rocks the ragged rascal ran' . . . and 'Methodist Episcopal.' "

LINEWEAVER *(Enters from GLANZ 's office and strides briskly across the ward)*   Okey dokey, guys, VD patients fall out for *short-arm inspection! (As the patients slowly assemble at the foot of their beds, he approaches MAGRUDER)* Magruder, Dr. Glanz wants to see you at eleven o'clock—to start your sexual profile. *(With abrupt sympathy)* He's got the results of yesterday's blood test on you. Your Wassermann has risen from a three positive to a four positive. Incredible! That's as positive as you can get. *(Honestly commiserating)* I'm sorry, sonny boy. I'm really sorry about that. It's soared clean out of sight. *(Turns back and goes to GLANZ 's office door)* VD patients all assembled for short-arm, sir!

GLANZ   Thank you, Lineweaver.

MAGRUDER *(Standing in a trance of anxiety now, gazing at SCHWARTZ)*   Each second, each minute, each hour: how they must be multiplying, those miserable little corkscrews! *(Pauses, then bursts out in a rage)* If I could *fight* this! If I could only *see* the enemy, I'd feel that I had a chance! But the little fuckers are deep inside me, burrowing away like a horde of hideous, microscopic *rats* and I can't get at them! *(Pauses)* And you know something else, Schwartz? You know what I feel? What I fear?

SCHWARTZ   What's that?

MAGRUDER   *Nothing's* going to get at them. No medicine! No cure! I'm going to end up a gibbering lunatic, screaming like a banshee in a padded cell. I can already *feel* those interminable days and nights—the horror!—my tongue no more able to grapple with speech than the tongue of a newborn baby. *(Pauses)* What are those words again, Schwartz?

SCHWARTZ   *(Reading)*   Let's see. Yes. "Truly rural."

MAGRUDER   *(Repeating the words, at first slowly, but then quickly and frantically)*   Truly rural . . . Truly rural.

SCHWARTZ   "Thirty-third artillery brigade."

MAGRUDER   Thirty-third artillery brigade!

SCHWARTZ   "Around the rough and rugged rocks the ragged rascal ran."

MAGRUDER   Around the rough and rugged rocks the ragged rascal ran!

SCHWARTZ   "Methodist Episcopal . . ."
       (The lights fade on the scene)

It is eleven o'clock the same morning. The scene is DR.
GLANZ *'s office.* MAGRUDER *stands at stiff attention outside the office
while* DR. GLANZ *explains the workings of a machine that sits on
the desk to* CAPTAIN BUDWINKLE.

GLANZ   This is a remarkable new gadget for recording the
human voice, sir. It has been distributed to a few select
specialists. It's called a wire recorder.

BUDWINKLE *(With great interest)*   Oh, yes, I've heard about
them.

GLANZ   Warfare is an amazing human activity, sir. On the
negative side, it does spawn social diseases such as the one
that has afflicted our misguided young patient outside.
(Nods toward MAGRUDER*)* But on the positive end of the
scale, the technological end, the benefits must be incalcu-
lable. Think of the possibilities, in the postwar years,
when a machine like this is simplified and refined, as it
surely will be. Think of the ease with which we will be
able imperishably to record the first cry of one's little
pink baby, or a presidential speech, or several hours of
uninterrupted inspiration from Dr. Norman Vincent
Peale.

BUDWINKLE   Outstanding! Ace of an idea! Tell me though,
Dr. Glanz, how is this machine applied in a practical
sense to venereal patients?

GLANZ   As you well know, sir, most venereal patients are inveterate liars, and the machine helps bend them in the direction of the truth. A patient will choose his words more carefully if he knows that his statements are subject to scrutiny ex post facto.

BUDWINKLE   Fascinating. What is your technique of interrogation?

GLANZ   You will begin to see in a moment, sir, with our young syphilitic, Magruder. Today we start in with the first of two phases. This phase we call the Overview.

BUDWINKLE   The Overwhat?

GLANZ   The Overview, sir. The Grand Design. The motivational, the behavioral, the biosociological aspects of a patient's sexual profile. It is only after dealing in the more abstract that we can get to the more specific, the second phase. This we call the Blitz phase. In the Blitz phase— if you'll permit us a small witticism, sir—we come to the real *crotch* of the matter. But first, today, the Overview. Magruder, come in and be seated! (MAGRUDER *enters the office and takes a seat opposite* GLANZ *and* BUDWINKLE) We assume that Lineweaver has told you the state of your Wassermann, boy.

MAGRUDER   Yes, sir.
      (GLANZ *turns on the recorder*)

GLANZ   It means that you are extremely virulent. Therefore you must take the utmost pains to be truthful with us while we record your history on this machine. If you do so meticulously, we may be able to try to save your life. Do you understand?

MAGRUDER   Yes, sir.

GLANZ *(Consults some notes)*   First, it is our recollection that you told us that you have had sexual congress with only quote two women unquote in quote my entire life unquote, these females being quote an older woman unquote and quote my girl unquote. Is this correct?

MAGRUDER   I think so, sir.

GLANZ   What do you mean, "I think so"?

MAGRUDER   I got lost in all those quotes. I mean—yes, sir, that's all correct.

GLANZ   Very well, what we want to know now is this. With whom did you have relations *first*—the older woman or the girl?

MAGRUDER   My girl, sir.

GLANZ *(Patiently)*   Now, Magruder, we don't mean for you to describe the actual *carnal connection* with this girl. That won't be necessary—at least for the moment. What we want you to do is to outline your early relationship with her, and the events leading up to the initial act of—coition. Tell us what it was that brought the two of you together in the first place. We assume it was some powerful erotic attraction.

MAGRUDER   No, sir. It was poetry.

GLANZ   Poetry?

MAGRUDER   Well, we certainly had a powerful erotic attraction for each other. But that wasn't really the important thing at all—not at first, at least. Like I say, it was poetry. The other came later.

GLANZ   Kindly explain.
    (He fiddles with the machine)

MAGRUDER   In high school we had this senior English class together, Ann—that's her name—and I. Well, we just fell into reading a lot of poetry together, out loud.

BUDWINKLE   What *kind* of poetry? *Porno* poetry? Of the Whitman ilk?

MAGRUDER   Well, sir, as a matter of fact—yes. Funny you said that, sir. Walt Whitman and Shakespeare and Keats and—

BUDWINKLE   *(Interrupting)* Shakespeare, Whitman and Keats. Three fat English faggots. That's a *fine* gaggle of fruitimatoots to inspire manliness in a man.

MAGRUDER   Whitman's an American, sir.

BUDWINKLE   Never mind, they're all faggots. In England everybody's queer. Even the *strawberries* are queer in England. Only one English poet escaped being a pederast, and that was Kipling. *(Recites in an orotund voice)* "Now these are the Laws of the Jungle / and many and mighty are they / But the head and the hoof of the Law / and the haunch and the hump / is—*Obey!*" If you had been exposed to more poetry like that, Magruder, you might not be in your present pickle.

GLANZ   Well said, sir. Continue, Magruder.

MAGRUDER   Well, sir, I guess it was one of those weekends we'd been reading poetry together—one Saturday afternoon it was. There'd been a rainstorm, and my girl and I—we'd had to run across some fields and hole up in an old broken-down tobacco barn . . . and it was on that afternoon that I realized that I was in love with her. And I guess I knew she was in love with me. It was the first time for me, the first time I had made love to anyone, and somehow it was all mixed up with this poetry we'd discovered together. I imagine you could say it was like a religious experience—

BUDWINKLE *(Interrupts)* I imagine *you* could say it was like a religious experience, young friend. Most Americans do not equate divine worship with the act of fornication.

GLANZ That's very nice, Magruder, very idyllic. Very religious. But from our viewpoint you've left out an important detail. *(Pauses)* At this time, was the girl a virgin?

MAGRUDER Oh, yes, sir. I'm positive she was.

GLANZ Very well. I can only take your word. This, then, was the beginning of an affair during which, by your own admission, you had physical relations quote many, many times unquote. What we now want to know is this: How long did this affair last?

MAGRUDER Well, sir, it's still going on, I guess you could say. But it *was* interrupted.

GLANZ Kindly explain.

MAGRUDER I went with Ann all through the next year, until the beginning of the following summer. Then she had to go away. Her parents went away for the summer, to the beach, and took Ann with them.

GLANZ And you were alone. *(Pauses)* Alone. Deprived of your customary means of sexual release.

MAGRUDER *(Darkly)* Well, in a manner of speaking, sir. If you want to put it that way.

GLANZ Are we correct in assuming, then, that it was sometime during this summer that you encountered the "older woman" you mentioned, with whom you had the heretofore-mentioned sexual relations?

MAGRUDER   That's right, sir.

GLANZ   Kindly describe those relations in detail—

BUDWINKLE   *(Interrupting)*   Just a minute, Doctor. *(To MA-GRUDER)* From all you have said, I take it you were very much in love with this girl of yours. Right?
   (He leans forward accusingly)

MAGRUDER   Yes, sir. Oh, yes, sir.

BUDWINKLE   I may be dense, Magruder. Obtuse. Stupid even. Feel free to correct me if I don't make sense. But one of the important aspects of love between man and woman is *fidelity*, is it not? Decks clean fore and aft, and all squared away amidships? *(Pauses)* I won't blow the whistle on you for having premarital relations, although that to my mind is a poisonous business. What I truly can't abide—and I want you to hear it loud and clear— is the idea that you betrayed this girl during her summer vacation!
   (He leans back in his chair, folds his arms with a look of consummate indignation)

MAGRUDER   *(Smarting badly under this assault, he nonetheless begins to protest)*   But, sir, if you'll let me try to ex- plain—

GLANZ   *(Severely)*   Then explain, Magruder! In detail!

MAGRUDER   That summer there wasn't much to do at night, and every now and then this friend of mine—his name was Roy Davis—he and I would get some beer and drive out in his father's car to this graveyard where it was quiet and dark, and we'd sit and talk. One night we were sitting there in the dark drinking beer, when this car came up next to us. There were a couple of older women in the car —it had been raining, but now the moon was out and we could see them in the moonlight—and they were laughing and drinking beer too. They were pretty drunk, really. Roy and I said hello and they said hello back, and we all laughed a lot, and pretty soon they came over and got into our car. They'd just finished working the night shift at the cotton mill. Some people in my hometown look down on these cotton mill workers and call them lintheads.

GLANZ   Lintheads?

MAGRUDER   Yes, sir. They work around these looms and machines, and the lint from the cotton gets into their hair and makes it look fuzzy. That's why they're called lintheads.

GLANZ   These women are of a lower social class then, would you not say so? Lower than your own, which from your fact sheet would seem to be middle-middle-middle.

MAGRUDER   Yes, sir, I guess you could say that.

GLANZ   Their names? No, both names won't be necessary. Just the name of *your*—linthead.

MAGRUDER   That's a funny thing, sir. I never knew her complete name, her first name. But I did hear Roy's older woman say to my older woman something like "That husband of yours! That mean ole thing, Tom Yancey!" So ever since that night I've always remembered her as Mrs. Yancey.

GLANZ   *(Into microphone)*   Mrs. Thomas Yancey. *(To MAGRUDER)*   What else happened?

MAGRUDER   There's not a whole lot else to say, sir—except that we got horsing around in the car, the four of us, and

I'd drunk quite a bit of beer, and I guess you might say that—well, I was pretty *horny*. In fact, I was good and horny! And Mrs. Yancey, she was all over me. Playing with me and all. Boy, was *she* horny! She just wouldn't stop! And she kept kissing me and messing with me and messing with me and got me all excited, and I began to mess with her and she got pretty excited, too. *(Pauses)* So, sir, Mrs. Yancey and I just got out of the car and went into the graveyard and I—I had relations with her. On top of a tombstone.

GLANZ   On top of a tombstone? Ye gods!

MAGRUDER   Yes, sir, because the ground was real wet. So we chose one of those, you know, horizontal tombstones. I remember it was on top of somebody—I guess you could literally say some body—named McCorkle.

GLANZ   And you had one single connection with this woman. Why only once, when your past history indicates such—how shall we call it?—such vigorous erotic propensities?

MAGRUDER   Because Mrs. Yancey passed out, sir. And besides, it began to rain again.

GLANZ   *(Makes notes, shuffles papers, and regards* MAGRUDER *for a long moment with great solemnity)*   And so, Magruder, as the Captain has just implied, after this clammy encounter —this sordid little romp of yours—you soon returned to the embrace of your beloved, this girl, with perfect calm and equanimity. Had you *no* sense of guilt at all?

MAGRUDER   Well, sir, in a way I did. But I've thought over that night many times. *(A long pause)* I got awfully horny that night. And it was only once. I felt maybe Ann might have understood. She's pretty understanding.

GLANZ Well, if you have no sense of guilt over this betrayal, perhaps you will be able to develop a sense of guilt over something far worse.

MAGRUDER What's that, sir?

GLANZ If, as you seem to have done, you took your girl's maidenhead, it would appear virtually impossible for her to have transmitted the disease to you. She would have been free from taint. So you obviously acquired your infection from this lower-class woman during your debauch that night in the cemetery. And the chances must be very close to one hundred percent that *you* in turn later transmitted the infection to this girl of yours.

MAGRUDER But, sir—

GLANZ No need to temporize, Magruder. The deed is done. Surely in the back of your *exceedingly* active mind there must have occurred that—that ugly probability.

MAGRUDER *(Frantically)* You mean—?

GLANZ *(Emphatically)* Yes. *(With a momentous pause)* That the disease that multiplies in you likewise multiplies *now* in that innocent, unsuspecting girl.

MAGRUDER Oh, Jesus! *(Pauses) Maybe* in the back of my mind! But to have somebody—I mean a doctor, *you*—say it like this—*(Cries out)* But I've never meant to hurt anyone! *No one!* Least of all—*her!*

BUDWINKLE Why are you crying, Magruder? For heaven's sake, stop it. *E-ech!* Crying in anyone over six makes my flesh crawl. Stop crying. I can't stand effeminacy.
    (MAGRUDER continues to weep silently, chin propped in his palms, gazing with despair into space beyond his hands)

GLANZ   Stop crying, Magruder, as the Captain commands
you! We insist you stop crying!

> (*He and* BUDWINKLE *stand over* MAGRUDER *now, exhorting him to cease crying, as he gazes into space, saying nothing, weeping helplessly. The scene ends in darkness, with* "We insist you stop crying!")

Act Three

It is several days later, mid-morning. MAGRUDER *sits alone, writing a letter. On the part of the ward near stage left a blackjack game is in progress. The players are* STANCIK, McDANIEL *and another. Their laconic cardplayers' dialogue—"Hit me," "I'll stick," "Hit me hard," etc.—is the first sound heard.* SCHWARTZ *is absent, while* CLARK *lies in his bed, with customary balefulness silently surveying the scene. In* DR. GLANZ'*s office,* LINEWEAVER *stands awaiting instructions from the doctor, who is seated at his desk.* MAGRUDER *puts his pen and paper down, rises and goes toward the head, stage left. As he walks, he trips clumsily and obviously over a bedpan on the floor, then recovers himself, exiting stage left.*

GLANZ   He'll be free to go Monday. (*Hands* LINEWEAVER *an envelope*) That'll be all for the moment, Lineweaver.

LINEWEAVER   Aye-aye, sir. (*Turns and leaves the office, walks onto the ward and approaches the blackjack players*) Stancik, I got good news for you. (STANCIK *and the other two look up*) Your dingdong doesn't leak any more, your smears for gonococci were negative, your prostate is peachy, your vas deferens is a dream, your urethra is adorable, your epididymus won the gold medal at the epididymus show —and you get out of here on Monday. Here are your marching orders.

STANCIK (*Exuberant*)   I told you I'd win that bet, McDaniel! I told you I'd beat that bug and be out of here by next week! Give me my five bucks!

McDANIEL *(Turning up a card)* Twenty-one. Pay me. *(Casually)* I'll deduct it from your blackjack account, Stancik. You owe me two hundred and twenty thousand dollars. Minus five.

LINEWEAVER Congratulations, Stancik.

STANCIK *(Looks at his orders)* It's really true. I'm gonna get out! *(Gazes into space with an exultant look)* I can't wait for my first liberty. I'm gonna go to Norfolk. Oh, man, I'm gonna go to Norfolk and shack up with this broad I met—

LINEWEAVER *(Interrupts)* I hope you have an independent income, Stancik. Because on account of the clap, and on account of how long it took to cure you, I calculate you've forfeited your pay until about five years from now. You'll be in hock for that spectacular dose of yours when the war's over and everybody else has gone home.

STANCIK Ah, Christ, I *forgot* about that!

LINEWEAVER As for talk about shacking up with any broad, Stancik, let me tell you, you're a real marvel, a *phenomenon*. You go against *Nature!* Ulcer patients can't bear to think about eating, guys with fallen arches shudder at the idea of having to walk, people with laryngitis—the *last* thing they want to do is to talk. Every patient I ever saw come on this ward gets so turned off sex you'd think they were eunuchs. But *you*, Stancik, you're incredible! I swear to God, I think you've been here since before the clap was discovered, yet day in and day out, rain or shine, with the ghastly wages of *venery* manifest on every hand, all I've ever heard you talk about is *ass*. I dunno, you're *stupefying*, a real tribute to the life force or something.
(While he is talking, MAGRUDER *reenters from stage left and trips over the same bedpan)*

MAGRUDER *(In a desperate whisper)* Methodist Episcopal!
(He goes to his chair and sinks down heavily, head in his hands)

LINEWEAVER *(Attention caught by* MAGRUDER, *he approaches him)* How you feeling, sonny boy?

MAGRUDER *(Despondently raises his head)* Yesterday's blood test? How was it?

LINEWEAVER Sorry, I wish I could bring you some cheer. But it's still holding the line right up there. *(Looks at him closely)* Are you really feeling all right? You look a bit feverish. *(Feels his brow)* Hmm. You're a little warm. I'll take your temperature in a minute. How are you feeling?

MAGRUDER Not very good, to be quite honest. All sort of achey and, you know, *blah*— And you know another thing? My gums have begun to bleed like crazy.

LINEWEAVER Open up. *(Inspects his gums)* Mmmh. Quite so. Rather inflamed.

MAGRUDER They're not bleeding now, but Jesus, whenever I brush my teeth—*(Halts, and there is a new edge of anxiety in his voice)* You don't really think that—I mean—*(Breaks off)* What do you think it means?

LINEWEAVER I dunno. I *just* don't know. We'd better have that checked out. *(He strides toward stage left, looking worried and preoccupied)* We'd just better have that checked out. *(He exits)*

CLARK *(Rises up on his elbow in bed, laughing his malicious little laugh)* It's dem *spiral*-keets. De *spiral*-keets, dey movin' right up. Dey in yo' mouf. Dat's how come you bleedin'. Dey movin' *right* up. Pretty soon dey gwine be *right* up yere. *(Grins as he points to his skull)* Den—*dat's* all! Tee-hee.

(MAGRUDER, *absorbing what* CLARK *says, glaring at him but ignoring him, sits down to write a letter. After a moment of writing, he suddenly crumples up the letter, hurls it across the ward, and rises in a rage*)

MAGRUDER (*Speaks in the direction of* CLARK, *but his anguish now is really voiced inward to himself*)   Yet I'm lying to her! Not only am I a sack of corruption, I'm a shameless, unspeakable liar! All because I don't have the courage, the guts to tell her the *truth*. (*Pauses, his agony growing more intense*) But the *truth!* How can you tell that kind of truth? How can you tell someone that you've filled them with some evil pollution? Jesus, I've *got* to tell her, but how do you find words for such hideous news? (*Pauses*) And that Goddamned Mrs. Yancey! I'd write her too if I knew her address! I'd write her and tell her to stop cruising around graveyards and contaminating people!

CLARK (*Slowly, passively, distantly*)   Dem *spiral*-keets. Dey is trouble. Dey is *baa-ad* trouble.

MAGRUDER (*Begins to write, tears up a sheet of paper, then repeats this action in despair. He then reaches into the pocket of his robe in search of his wallet, frantically pats the other pocket, finds the wallet gone*)   My wallet! (*To* CLARK) My wallet! My wallet with her pictures! (*Begins to dig around in his seabag, looks under the mattress and under the bed*) My wallet! It's gone!

CLARK   How much money you done had in dere, white boy?

MAGRUDER   I don't know. Not much. (*His voice becomes distraught*) Not much! Five dollars, maybe six. But it's not the money. It's her pictures! Those snapshots of my girl. There were three of them. And they're gone!

CLARK *(Beckons to him)* Come here. I want tell you some-thin'. *(His voice becomes conspiratorial as* MAGRUDER *approaches)* Listen close while I tells you somethin'.

MAGRUDER *(Wildly impatient)* What?

CLARK Somebody *took* dat wallet, and I seed it wid mah own eyes.

MAGRUDER Well *who*, then? *Who* took it?

CLARK De Jew-boy took it!

MAGRUDER *(Draws back, incredulous)* Schwartz? Schwartz took my wallet? You're crazy, Lorenzo! Crazy! Schwartz wouldn't steal anyone's wallet!

CLARK I'm *tellin'* you! Swear befo' God three times and hopes I goes straight to *hell* if'n dat Jew-boy didn't steal you' wallet. *(His voice, though enervated, is filled with passion and conviction)* It were *he!*

MAGRUDER *(Still incredulous, but weakening)* When did you see Schwartz steal my wallet, Lorenzo? Don't lie about this. I know you hate him, but don't accuse some innocent man!

CLARK He stole hit las' night. In de dead of night I seed him grab it. Awake all night I was, jest a-lyin' here with my eyes cracked open, and I seed de Jew-boy git up to go to de head. Den by an' by he come back, and he seed dat wallet in yo' robe hangin' dere, and he *tuk* it. He tuk it clean on out'n dat robe and carried it wid him to bed. Dat is a Jew thief!

MAGRUDER *(Weakening further)* I can't believe this. *(Pauses)* I just can't believe that somebody like Schwartz would steal anyone's wallet.
    (He continues to search around his bed)

CLARK *(His voice intimate, confidential)* Hit well known. One thing. De Jew peoples *do* like money—

MAGRUDER *(Protesting)* Oh, come on, Lorenzo. That's an old, ridiculous—

CLARK *(Interrupting)* Let me ax you somethin'! Who else dey *is* to steal it but de Jew-boy? *(Gestures to the three beds)* Dere *you* is. Dere *he* is. Here *I* is. An' *I*—I can't move any inch. We de only ones dis end ob de hospital. So ain't no one but de Jew-boy *could* steal it. Hee-hee! Less'n you gone steal it yo'self.

MAGRUDER *(Pauses, deeply perplexed, but beginning to see some logic in this)* But I just can't accept the idea that someone like Schwartz—

CLARK *(Interrupts again, angrily)* I doesn't *lie*, white boy. Enough! Believe me or believe me not! I don't keer!
    (CLARK rolls over weakly. During his last speech, SCHWARTZ has appeared at stage left. As CLARK rolls over, SCHWARTZ moves across the ward toward MAGRUDER. Walking, he displays a new quality of debilitation, exemplified in a certain slow, halting feebleness of gait)

SCHWARTZ Hello, Wally. How you feelin', Wally?

MAGRUDER *(With a certain stiffness and coolness)* Not so good, thank you.

SCHWARTZ *(In an offhand way, devoid of self-pity, as he fumbles for something in his seabag)* Well, with me it's very much the same as you. I had another examination this morning. You know these pains I began to have the other night? *(Looks fearfully up at MAGRUDER)* They think my condition has spread now. Spread. *(Pauses)* Spreading!

MAGRUDER *(Cool, stiffly polite)*   Schwartz, I've got to ask you something.

SCHWARTZ   Certainly, Wally. What is it?

MAGRUDER   Have you seen my wallet? It's missing.

SCHWARTZ   Your wallet? You mean, have I ever seen your wallet? Why, yes, I saw it the other day. When you were looking at those pictures of your girl.

MAGRUDER   No, not *then*. I mean since last night.

SCHWARTZ   No, Wally, I honestly can't say that I have.

MAGRUDER   Schwartz, I hate to— I've got to ask you something. Did you take my wallet?

SCHWARTZ   *(So dumbfounded that he can barely speak for a moment)*   Did I steal your wallet? *Did I steal your wallet!*

MAGRUDER   *(Wildly agitated now)*   Not steal! I said *take!* I'm not accusing you of stealing it. Only taking it. Taking it, see? Taking it maybe because you wanted to borrow five dollars to go to the PX this morning and didn't want to wake me up to ask for it. Something like that. I'm not accusing you of *stealing* it, only taking it. But now I want it back! Where is it, Schwartz? I want that wallet back!

SCHWARTZ   *(In anguish)*   No! I didn't *touch* your wallet! What are you saying? I've never stolen a thing in my life. *(He advances resentfully on* MAGRUDER, *pressing close)* Except for that fuckin' *book*, which I stole *for you!*

MAGRUDER   *(Edging away but still furious)*   Quit breathing on me. Admit you *stole* that wallet!

SCHWARTZ   I'm *not* breathing on you. *(Coming even closer)* And I didn't steal your fuckin' wallet! Only somebody

like *you*—some dirty, degenerate *Southern-born cracker* would accuse an innocent man of something like that!
(They advance on each other, fists clenched)

CLARK *(Suddenly interrupting)* Hey, Jew-boy! *Tolerance!* Hee-hee!
(On this last outburst, LINEWEAVER has entered from stage left, and immediately rushes to break up the fracas)

LINEWEAVER   Break it up! Break it up! What's going on here? No fighting among the invalids. Dr. Glanz's orders. *(He interposes himself between the two, gently pushing MAGRUDER back and away)* Interesting idea, though. The first matched bout between syphilis and consumption. *(Adds to MA-GRUDER, almost as an afterthought)* Take it easy, sonny boy. Oh, they found this wallet of yours at the hospital laundry. *(Hands him the wallet)* It was in your other robe. There's some honesty left, even in the U.S. Navy.
(He exits stage right. There is a long silence, pregnant with a sense of humiliation)

MAGRUDER   You've got to forgive me, Schwartz. How can I ever apologize for saying what I said to you just now? *(Turns toward CLARK's bed)* And you! You, Lorenzo. You're a black no-good nigger son of a bitch.

CLARK   Hee-hee!

SCHWARTZ *(Sitting down weakly)* Don't, Wally! It's no use calling him names. I should have known that he was at the bottom of it all. I had forgotten what he was capable of. *(Turns to CLARK)* But, oh, Clark, you're an evil *schwarze*. I've never known anyone as evil as you.

CLARK   Hee-hee!

SCHWARTZ   Clark!

CLARK   What do you want, Jew-boy?

SCHWARTZ *(At white heat)*   Hey, listen, Clark, why can't you ever once call me by my real name? I mean, that's not so much to ask, is it? I call you by *your* real name. I don't call you nigger. I call you *Clark*, you nigger! (CLARK *laughs*) Oh, boy, Clark, if there ever lived a nigger who deserved to be called a nigger, you, Clark, are that nigger, you *nigger!*

CLARK   Jew-boy don' like to be called a Jew-boy, 'cause de Jew-boy *is* a Jew-boy, and who wants to be a Jew-boy?

MAGRUDER   I'm sorry about it all, Schwartz. Sorry from the bottom of my heart. I hope you'll accept my apology.

SCHWARTZ   You don't have to apologize, Wally. I understand. I'm sorry too for what *I* said. *(Pauses and gazes about him, as if to emphasize, silently, his hatred and fear of the place)* When—when you accused me just now, I could only think all of a sudden, "It's his sickness that's making him do that." I said to myself, "Remember? That's all part of his sickness."

MAGRUDER *(With dawning apprehension)*   What do you mean? What do you mean, Schwartz—all part of my sickness?

SCHWARTZ   Nothing, Wally.

MAGRUDER *(With great anxiety)*   Tell me what you meant by that!

SCHWARTZ *(Placatingly)*   Really nothing, Wally. Nothing. Nothing at all.

MAGRUDER   You mean about the money? And what it said in that book?

SCHWARTZ (*Reluctantly*) Well, yes—

MAGRUDER What did the book say?

SCHWARTZ Wally, Wally, don't *torment* yourself.

MAGRUDER But what did it say? *You* remember.

SCHWARTZ It said something like, When you've got paresis, one of the first signs is the patient's suspicion that other people are intent on stealing from him.

MAGRUDER (*Sits down slowly, with a stunned and frightened look*) My God, yes. I'd forgotten that. Oh, my God! (*Turns to* CLARK) But I had good cause! I mean, Lorenzo there—he was behind it all. (*Pauses*) Even so! I wouldn't have said that to you if I wasn't sick! (*Pauses again with a look of terror, then thrusts his hands against his forehead*) Like Dr. Glanz said, it's gone to my brain! I'm mad! Stark raving mad! Stark raving mad! Stark raving mad! Stark raving mad!

(*Pandemonium erupts. He goes into a delirium, and has to be controlled and placated. The lights fade*)

It is several days later, mid-morning. MAGRUDER *is absent.*
CLARK *is absent too, his bed freshly made-up and empty.* SCHWARTZ
*is in bed for the first time, lying with a thermometer in his mouth
as he reads his book* How to Manage a Pet Shop. *As the scene
opens,* LINEWEAVER *strides across the ward from stage left and stops
at* SCHWARTZ*'s bed to examine the thermometer.*

LINEWEAVER   Hmm. Not bad. How do you feel this morning, old pal?

SCHWARTZ *(Strokes his abdominal area)*   The pain's not there
so much now. Not like last night. That was terrible!

LINEWEAVER   Did that shot I gave you help any?

SCHWARTZ   Oh, yes, I went fast asleep. It took the pain right
away. And, you know, I had these wonderful dreams.
Fantastic dreams! Dreams filled with all sorts of animals.
Funny, it must come from reading my book here, about
running a pet shop.

LINEWEAVER *(Feeling* SCHWARTZ*'s pulse)*   That's good. Good
to have the pain go away and dream nice dreams.

SCHWARTZ   In one of them I dreamed I was in this pet shop
I'm going to buy after the war's over. Only it's strange,
you know, there weren't any cages. The animals—they
were all running around free. *(Pauses)* What a funny
dream. Anyone knows you can't have a pet shop without
cages.

LINEWEAVER *(Abstractedly)* Mmm-hmm. Strange thing about dreams. What's your pleasure, Schwartz? You'd like some orange juice? How about some orange juice with a lot of crushed ice?

SCHWARTZ Yeah, that might be nice.

LINEWEAVER *(Moves away)* I'll have it sent up from the galley. *(At extreme stage left he encounters* ANDERSON, *one of the hospital corpsmen, and speaks to him out of* SCHWARTZ'S *hearing. To indicate the gravity of* SCHWARTZ'S *condition, he makes a series of nervous jabbing downward motions with his thumb)* I don't know if that morphine has worn off or not. If he begins to hurt again, give him eight more milligrams I.V.

> *(He exits. For a moment* SCHWARTZ *continues to read, then* MAGRUDER *enters stage right, carrying his seabag. He still wears the robe with its embroidered "S")*

MAGRUDER Hi, Schwartz.

SCHWARTZ *(Looking up)* Wally! Welcome back! I thought you were gone for good.

MAGRUDER No, Schwartz, no such luck. It was my gums. Remember how my gums were bleeding? They put me upstairs on the observation ward for four days and gave me a lot of dental treatment. Guess what they found out? *(Pauses)* Trench mouth. I had trench mouth.

SCHWARTZ So now you're back.

MAGRUDER So now I'm back.

SCHWARTZ Back.

MAGRUDER Back. *(Long pause)* Anyway, they cured my trench mouth. They put some purple medicine on my gums that made me look like a Ubangi, and it cleared up in forty-eight hours. *(Pauses)* Wonderful, pure mouth I've got now. Clean and trouble-free. A mouth any girl would love to kiss. If she didn't know what else I had. *(Pauses again, looks around)* Where's Lorenzo?

SCHWARTZ   Clark? *(Silence for a moment)* He's dead.

MAGRUDER   *Dead? (Another silence)* I can't believe it! Jesus!

SCHWARTZ   He went fast, Wally. How long have you been gone? Four days? He must have—died on Tuesday, the second day after you left. Just after you went upstairs he fell into this kind of stupor, I guess you'd call it. Dr. Glanz and Lineweaver and everybody tried to bring him around, but it was no use. *(Pauses)* Boy, did he smell bad toward the end!

MAGRUDER *(Brooding)*   It's sad. Hateful as he was, it's sad. I guess it always is. *(Pauses)* It's hard to believe. Lorenzo's dead.

SCHWARTZ   It *was* sad. I couldn't help feeling terribly sorry for him when he went into that stupor—even after all the ugly and vicious things he's said. *(Pauses)* You know, Wally, I felt so sorry for him that I had to try to communicate with him. His face turned kind of blue—a strange deep kind of blue like ink welling up through his black skin—and his lips curled back from his teeth in this awful look of agony. It wrenched something out of me—out of my heart. He seemed so alone in his dying. So helpless.

MAGRUDER   Did you say anything to him? Did you get *to* him somehow?

SCHWARTZ   In a way, I guess you'd say. But not really, even though I tried. I don't know, Wally, as I got up and looked at him, looking at that fuckin' agony on his face, and watching him breathe in this tortured way, I said to my-self, "Well, he's dying." And so I looked in Rabbi Weinberg's book, in the index, under D for Death. And I read Lorenzo that wonderful line that goes like this: "Dying is a beautiful and natural part of the life process, no more to be feared than sleep." And I heard Lorenzo say, very softly: "Dat is mule shit." Then I said to myself, "This hatred of his, it's only because of the hatred that we in turn—we whose skins are white—have poured out on *him*. I thought I should ask Lorenzo to forgive me—to forgive us—for all we've done to him, so I looked in the book under Forgiveness and read that fantastic thought that goes: "The most noble of human gifts is the gift of forgiveness." And then I said, "Don't you understand, Lorenzo? Can't you forgive me?" And his voice was so terribly weak and faint. I heard him say, "Forgiveness." And he gave that funny little laugh and said again, "Forgiveness. Dat do grab my black ass." *(Pauses)* Wally, Wally, I was desperate! He was fading there, dying right in front of my eyes. I felt that I just *couldn't* let him go with this hatred all bottled up inside him. Somehow I just *had* to reach him with the message of brotherhood. So I read that passage in the book where the Rabbi quotes from Beethoven's Ninth Symphony *"Alle Menschen werden Bruder"*—I hope I'm pronouncing it right—"All mankind become brothers when they join hands and love one another." Then I stopped reading and I looked down at him and said: "Lorenzo, we mustn't live and die with this awful hate inside us. We must be brothers and love one another." Then at last I said, "I love you, Lorenzo. I love you as a brother. Please allow yourself to love me in return." *(Pauses)* And finally he spoke—so faint and weak —they must have been almost the last words he said. And you know what they were? *(Pauses)* He said, "Yes, I'll love you. *(Pauses)* "Yes*, I'll love you! I will love you, Jew-boy. I will love you when the Lord makes roses bloom in a pig's asshole."

(At this moment the light goes up in the office of DR. GLANZ, *who in pantomine begins to converse with* LINEWEAVER *)*

MAGRUDER *(After pondering* SCHWARTZ*'s words)* Well, he stuck by his guns to the end. You have to give him that. *(Pauses)* And you, Schwartz. How are things with you?

SCHWARTZ *(Makes a little "like-this-like-that" gesture with his hand)* Oh, I don't know, Wally, I've had better days. But it's good to see you. Even though I know you're not glad *you're* back.

MAGRUDER *(Mournfully)* No, Schwartz, I'm not glad I'm back.

SCHWARTZ *(Tentatively)* Had any—had any bad symptoms?

MAGRUDER No. *(Pauses)* Well, I don't know. I tripped again the other day, and I thought—locomotor ataxia! I was in a terrible sweat all that day, but it didn't come back. *(Pauses)* I don't know, Schwartz. By now I'm pretty well resigned to whatever's got to come.

SCHWARTZ You look *fine*, Wally. I wouldn't worry about a stumble like that. Your legs are all wobbly from too little exercise, that's all. You really look fine. I wish I felt as healthy as you look.

MAGRUDER If I looked like I felt you'd see a syphilitic marine of a hundred and six.

SCHWARTZ *(In some pain now, he makes a small groan)* Aaah-h!

MAGRUDER What's wrong? Do you need—

SCHWARTZ It's nothing. It comes and goes, the pain. I'll be all right.

LINEWEAVER *(Enters from stage left, where he has been talking with* DR. GLANZ *)* Magruder, you're going to help Uncle

Sugar win the war after all. Both of the Wassermann tests you had on the observation ward were totally negative.

MAGRUDER *(Stupefied)*   What on earth are you talking about?

LINEWEAVER   It turns out you're clean as a whistle. You've got no more syphilis than Mickey Mouse.

MAGRUDER   I don't know what you mean!

LINEWEAVER   Your diagnosis has been changed to a false positive Wassermann due to trench mouth.

MAGRUDER   Some kind of joke. *(Bursts out in a rage)* No jokes, Lineweaver! None of your smartass jokes! I can't *take* anything like that, hear me!

LINEWEAVER *(Grasps him by the arms to calm him)*   It's not a joke, sonny boy! You'll live to die a hero on a wonderful Pacific beach somewhere. That's a lot better, isn't it, than ending up with the blind staggers, or in the booby hatch? And if you really die with enough dash and style, they might even give you the Navy Cross.

MAGRUDER *(Still stunned)*   But I don't understand!

LINEWEAVER   Simple. Let me explain. The Wassermann test is almost foolproof. In rare cases, however—once in thousands of times—some other disease will turn up a false reaction. Malaria is one, for instance. Trench mouth's another. When the dental surgeon cured your trench mouth, your Wassermann went negative—plop!— just like that.

MAGRUDER *(Breaking away from his grasp)*   What are you saying, Lineweaver? Do you realize what you're saying?

LINEWEAVER *(Cajolingly)*   I'd better let the boss man say the rest, sonny boy. Dr. Glanz'll explain. He wants to see you right now. Oh, by the way, here are your orders. You can report back to your outfit tomorrow.

(He hands him his orders)

MAGRUDER *(Still in a state of shock, wrestling with this new knowledge like a man reprieved from a death sentence, he walks dazedly to* DR. GLANZ *'s office)* Negative Wassermann? False Positive! *Trench mouth!*

(He pauses in front of DR. GLANZ *'s door, and it is immediately apparent from his suddenly rigid stance that he is aware of what is going on within. At this point, our attention is caught by* DR. GLANZ, *who sits silently before the wire recorder in his office, in deep contemplation, listening to his own interview with* MAGRUDER; *the expression on his face is sensual, flushed, unabashedly erotic)*

GLANZ'S VOICE Blitz phase. Session number two. *(Pause)* Now, Magruder, we want to remind you again that you must describe your physical relations with the girl in your very own words, repeat, *your very own words.* Now then *(Pauses)*—Did the nipples of her breasts grow pink and excited when you stroked them with your hand?

MAGRUDER'S VOICE *(In a tone of protest)* Well, sir—*(Pauses)* Yes, sir, they *did*, but—

GLANZ'S VOICE *(Sternly)* In your own words, Magruder! We *insist* on your own words!

MAGRUDER'S VOICE Well, sir, then yes. The nipples of her breasts grew pink and excited when I stroked them with my hand.

(GLANZ stops the machine and plays back twice the last sentence above, then lets the machine run on)

GLANZ'S VOICE And her thighs. Were they warm and smooth when you caressed them?

MAGRUDER'S VOICE   Yes, sir, her thighs were warm and smooth when I caressed them.

(*The recorder clicks off and* MAGRUDER *enters the office, his fists clutched in fury*)

GLANZ (*Suddenly flustered*)   The Scottish people have an ancient saying, our boy: "The best laid schemes of mice and man aft gang aglay." Do you know what that implies? Have you heard that saying?

MAGRUDER (*Slowly, trancelike, almost mesmerized, with the first seeds of rage being sown in his mind*)   It's not an ancient saying. It's from a poem by Robert Burns. Sir. (*The "Sir" is added following a pause, almost as an afterthought*) And it's "gang aft aglay."

GLANZ   At any rate, you may understand the implication. It is relevant, also, to our modern scientific marvels. The best-made instruments of medical research and diagnosis do, from time to time, gang slightly aglay. The Wassermann test is an example. Superb a tool as it is for detecting disease, it is not infallible. In your case, regrettably, it did prove fallible.

MAGRUDER (*His voice a tentative murmur*)   Then why didn't you tell me—

GLANZ (*Not hearing his beginning protest*)   As Lineweaver has doubtless told you, your positive reaction was caused by the latent trench mouth which you had when you took your first blood test and which erupted full-blown while you were here. The causative organisms—the spirochetes of trench mouth and syphilis—are quite similar. While this reaction rarely happens, it *does* happen—

MAGRUDER (*The voice still remote, but growing stronger*)   You could have *told* me.

GLANZ   What say, Magruder?

MAGRUDER   (*Very loud now*)   You could have—*told* me!

GLANZ   (*Slightly rattled by his tone*)   Told you what?

MAGRUDER   (*His words very precise and measured in his rage, which is barely controlled now*)   Told me what you just told me now.

GLANZ   We don't quite understand—

MAGRUDER   (*Frankly aggressive now, heedless of his subordinate position*)   Then I'll try to *make* you understand. If what you say is true you could have given me some *hope*. You could have told me that I *might* have had some other disease. Latent trench mouth. Athlete's foot! Ringworm! Something else! Anything! You could have been less god-damned certain that I was going to *die* full of paresis and locomotor ataxia!

GLANZ   (*Alarmed by* MAGRUDER'*s tone, rises from his chair*)   Mind your tone, Magruder. We're in authority here! The reason we failed to give you such information is because it is our firm policy never falsely to arouse a patient's expectations, his hopes—

MAGRUDER   (*Fully exercised now, he advances in a fury on the doctor, circling the corner of his desk*)   Hope! What do you know about hope and expectations! Don't talk to me about hope and expectations, you wretched son of a bitch!

GLANZ   You're insubordinate, Magruder! You'll get a court-martial for this! You're speaking to a lieutenant commander in the United States Navy!

MAGRUDER   (*Coming closer to* GLANZ, *who is now plainly frightened, he seizes a light metal chair and brandishes it at the doctor much as a lion tamer would*)   Pipe down, you hear! *I'm* going to have something to say now. Don't give me any of the lieutenant-commander crap! To me you're some kind of terrible Gauleiter. The only difference between you and an SS man is that an SS man doesn't stink of chloroform. Give me that recording, you filthy sadistic pig!

GLANZ *(In a panic now)* Magruder, you must have taken leave of your senses! Desist, we say! Leave off! *(In the direction of the door)* Corporal of the Guard! *(To* MAGRUDER *)* We protest this—this—

MAGRUDER *(Interrupting him, he drops the chair and pinions* GLANZ *to the wall by the neck)* Don't give me any more of this "we" shit, either! You're not Congress, or some god-damned corporation, or the King of Sweden! You're a loathsome little functionary with a dirty mind and a ste-thoscope, and goddamn you, from now on I insist you say *I*—like niggers, Jews and syphilitics! Give me that re-cording!

GLANZ *(Trying desperately to appease him)* Magruder, boy, stop! Let us explain. Ow! You're hurting us! Let us try to explain. Ow! Ow! You might fracture our hyoid bone!

MAGRUDER *Me!* Not *us!* Say let *me* try to explain, dammit.

GLANZ *(Acquiescing in a choked voice)* Let *me* try to explain. Ow! Ow! You're compressing our submaxillary gland!

MAGRUDER *(Still attacking, with his hands grasping the doctor's neck, he roughly shoves* GLANZ *down into his own chair)* Start explaining!

GLANZ   First, we want to say—

MAGRUDER   "*I*" want to say—

GLANZ   First I want to ask you—

MAGRUDER Hold it, Glanz! *I'm* going to ask the questions around here now. Listen again. Answer me. Tell me once more why it was you didn't let me know that there was a possibility—a *chance*, no matter how remote—of my being sick from something else.

GLANZ Because, as I said, it has always been our—*my* policy never to falsely arouse a patient's hopes. Ow! You're hurting my trachea!

MAGRUDER You lie, Glanz. It's because you got your jollies that way. That's the way you got your kicks!

GLANZ That's unfair, Magruder! Unfair! I am a *healer.* I have taken the Hippocratic oath. It would have been cruel to arouse in you unfounded expectations—

MAGRUDER *(Breaking in)* You're not a healer, Glanz! You're a ghoul. You feed off the very dregs of death.

GLANZ *(Struggling to get free again)* That's a slander, a vile slander! As a dedicated urologist sworn to alleviate human suffering I resent these canards, these accusations—

MAGRUDER *(Forcing him back down)* Pipe down, you creep! There's just a little bit more for me to say, and to hear you say; then you can serve me up to your policemen, your brig apes. There's something else I want to know. These *profiles* of yours, those miserable . . . filthy . . . pornographic examinations. What about them, Glanz? What purpose did they serve, except to jerk off and titillate that dirty mind of yours? Oh, I want that recording. I want somebody else to hear you at your work!

GLANZ *(Howls with chagrin)* Unfair again, Magruder. Foul! A foul aspersion! Without a biography in depth such as I took of you I should never have properly located your disease as having emanated from that older woman . . . with . . . whom *(Begins to realize what he is saying, and his voice fades)* you . . . had . . . relations. *(Pauses)* I never would have . . . pinpointed . . . the . . . uh . . . *source* . . . *(Halts)* I mean, Magruder—

(There is a prolonged silence now as they gaze at each other intently, the revelation in GLANZ *'s words creating an unspoken understanding)*

It is the same day, several hours later. MAGRUDER *sits on the chair by his bed, writing a letter. Dressed in a khaki shirt and pants, he is guarded by a* MARINE CORPORAL, *with an MP brassard and billy club, who stands nearby.* LINEWEAVER *enters from stage left to examine* SCHWARTZ, *who lies listlessly in bed in a half-doze.*

LINEWEAVER   How's everything, Schwartz?

SCHWARTZ *(After a pause)*   Better, I think. Those shots— they work.

LINEWEAVER *(Pats his shoulder)*   Good man. *(Turns away from* SCHWARTZ, *and approaching* MAGRUDER, *stands above him with his hands on his hips, addressing him rather like a parent to a wayward offspring)* Sonny boy, you got yourself into real trouble, didn't you? *(To the* MARINE CORPORAL*)* When do you take him to the brig?

MARINE CORPORAL   Any time now, I guess. I've gotta wait for Captain Budwinkle to finish writing out his report on the prisoner.

LINEWEAVER   Oh, you got yourself into *real* trouble, sonny boy. You might have committed murder or *sodomy*, or you might have run your ship aground on a reef—there are many terrible crimes in the naval service. But to have done what you did! To assault a superior officer! Oh, baby doll, the mind boggles at what they're going to do to you!

MAGRUDER *(Without emotion, and with exaggeratedly polite curiosity)* What's that, Lineweaver? What *are* they going to do?

LINEWEAVER   Well, when a sailor or a marine does something truly bad they send him to a big prison up in Portsmouth, New Hampshire. I'm sure you've heard of it. For what you did there's a special place *underneath* that prison where they bury you and throw away the key. *(In an aggrieved tone)* Why did you do it, Wally? How could you have done such an incredible thing?

MAGRUDER *(After a moment's contemplation)*   It wasn't incredible, Lineweaver. It's the only thing I could have done.

LINEWEAVER   Wally, just between the two of us, you *did* give Dr. Glanz a terrible scare. He was so upset that I had to give him three grains of Nembutal. Funny, he went off to sleep in his quarters all curled up shivering as if he had a chill and sucking his thumb like a baby. I never saw anything like it. *(Pauses)* And you know another thing?

MAGRUDER   What's that?

LINEWEAVER   It never happened before. I mean, he spoke to me in the first person singular. He said "I"—not *"we"*— he said . . . *"I-I* gotta go to bed!" *(Shakes his head)* Fantastic! *(He exits, stage left. MAGRUDER sits down to write his letter. As he writes, the portable radio plays music, interrupted by a brief news broadcast announcing large victories by General MacArthur's army forces in the South Pacific. Finally he puts the letter into an envelope, seals it and looks up at SCHWARTZ)*

MAGRUDER   How's it going, Schwartz? Feeling any better?

SCHWARTZ   Yeah, Wally. The shots, they make me feel better.

MAGRUDER   That's great. I'm betting my money you're out of here in a week.

SCHWARTZ   Maybe, Wally. Maybe so. Anyway, *you're* getting out of here. That's for sure. You're a fuckin' lucky man.

MAGRUDER   Yeah, Schwartz. I guess I am lucky. I guess anyone who gets out of here is lucky. You know, even going to the brig and all—a court-martial, prison, *anything* after this—I couldn't care less, really. It'll seem like being set free! *(He draws close to* SCHWARTZ*'s bed)* And you know another thing, Schwartz? Whatever else, I think I've gotten rid of my hypochondria. Breathe on me, Schwartz! *(With a faint smile,* SCHWARTZ *exhales in his face)* Fantastic. The breath of a babe! It was like a zephyr!
    *(*LINEWEAVER *enters from stage left and approaches the* MARINE CORPORAL *with some papers; the latter gives them a brief glance, then comes toward* MAGRUDER*)*

MARINE CORPORAL   All right, marine, grab your seabag and let's get going.

LINEWEAVER   Write me a letter from Portsmouth. I'm going to miss you, sonny boy. *(As* MAGRUDER *and the* CORPORAL *exit, he goes to* SCHWARTZ*'s bedside. He looks down at him, then sits on the edge of the bed and picks up the pet shop book)* Where were you reading, Schwartz?

SCHWARTZ *(Very weakly)*   I think it was the small dogs I was reading about. Yeah, the small dogs.

LINEWEAVER *(Begins to read as, very slowly, the sound of "There's a Star-Spangled Banner Waving Somewhere" rises up and over his voice)*   "Dollar-wise and pound for pound, the friendly, frolicsome Chihuahua is one of the most attractive items in the pet shop inventory. Another lovable little bundle of fun from south of the border is the frisky Mexican Hairless. Women will comprise most of your customers for these small breeds, as they may be carried about in handbags and are great to fondle and cuddle, satisfying the maternal instinct. Many times I have been asked the question by prospective pet shop owners: Aren't these small breeds more edgy and nervous than the larger dogs? My answer is an unqualified no. As a veterinarian with over thirty years of experience in handling all the canine varieties, I can testify that the notion of smaller dogs being more neurotic is strictly a myth . . ."

VINTAGE INTERNATIONAL

VINTAGE INTERNATIONAL

VINTAGE INTERNATIONAL

___ **By Grand Central Station I Sat Down and Wept** $10.00   0-679-73804-5
     by Elizabeth Smart
___ **Ake: The Years of Childhood** by Wole Soyinka $11.00   0-679-72540-7
___ **Ìsarà: A Voyage Around "Essay"** $9.95   0-679-73246-2
     by Wole Soyinka
___ **Children of Light** by Robert Stone $10.00   0-679-73593-3
___ **A Flag for Sunrise** by Robert Stone $12.00   0-679-73762-6
___ **Confessions of Nat Turner** by William Styron $12.00   0-679-73663-8
___ **Lie Down in Darkness** by William Styron $12.00   0-679-73597-6
___ **The Long March** and **In the Clap Shack** $11.00   0-679-73675-1
     by William Styron
___ **Set This House on Fire** by William Styron $12.00   0-679-73674-3
___ **Sophie's Choice** by William Styron $13.00   0-679-73637-9
___ **This Quiet Dust** by William Styron $12.00   0-679-73596-8
___ **Confessions of Zeno** by Italo Svevo $12.00   0-679-72234-3
___ **Ever After** by Graham Swift $11.00   0-679-74026-0
___ **Learning to Swim** by Graham Swift $9.00   0-679-73978-5
___ **Out of This World** by Graham Swift $10.00   0-679-74032-5
___ **Shuttlecock** by Graham Swift $10.00   0-679-73933-5
___ **The Sweet-Shop Owner** by Graham Swift $10.00   0-679-73980-7
___ **Waterland** by Graham Swift $11.00   0-679-73979-3
___ **The Beautiful Mrs. Seidenman** $9.95   0-679-73214-4
     by Andrzej Szczypiorski
___ **Diary of a Mad Old Man** by Junichiro Tanizaki $10.00   0-679-73024-9
___ **The Key** by Junichiro Tanizaki $10.00   0-679-73023-0
___ **On the Golden Porch** by Tatyana Tolstaya $10.00   0-679-72843-0
___ **The Eye of the Story** by Eudora Welty $8.95   0-679-73004-4
___ **Losing Battles** by Eudora Welty $10.00   0-679-72882-1
___ **The Optimist's Daughter** by Eudora Welty $9.00   0-679-72883-X
___ **The Passion** by Jeanette Winterson $10.00   0-679-72437-0
___ **Sexing the Cherry** by Jeanette Winterson $9.00   0-679-73316-7

Available at your bookstore or call toll-free to order: 1-800-733-3000.
Credit cards only. Prices subject to change.